MEMORIES
OF
LASTING SHADOWS

MEMORIES
OF
LASTING SHADOWS

MICHAEL GRYBOSKI

AMBASSADOR INTERNATIONAL
GREENVILLE, SOUTH CAROLINA & BELFAST, NORTHERN IRELAND

www.ambassador-international.com

Memories of Lasting Shadows

ISBN: 978-1-64960-079-0
eISBN: 978-1-64960-090-5
Library of Congress Control Number: 2020947134

Scripture quotations taken from The King James Version, The Authorized Version.

AMBASSADOR INTERNATIONAL
Emerald House
411 University Ridge, Suite B14
Greenville, SC 29601, USA
www.ambassador-international.com

AMBASSADOR BOOKS
The Mount
2 Woodstock Link
Belfast, BT6 8DD, Northern Ireland, UK
www.ambassadormedia.co.uk

The colophon is a trademark of Ambassador, a Christian publishing company.

"Indeed, if history shows anything, it is the failure of past generations to predict which aspects of their moral life future generations will find intolerable."

—COLIN KIDD,

Scottish historian

CHAPTER 1

"LET US PRAY," BEGAN THE chaplain in the echoing chamber of the United States Senate, his order prompting the bows of many elected heads and the closing of many established eyes. "Eternal Father, Who is ever present in our times of trouble and need, chaos and uncertainty, we give You thanks for the United States of America. For the blessings of living in a land of liberty and freedom for which we can worship You freely and without fear of persecution. We give thanks for this elected body of Congress, the Senate. Protect, guide, direct, and bless the business they bring in this new session. Let Your Spirit of unity remind us to love one another, to seek common cause in advancing Your kingdom . . . "

Roberta Sheridan reverently waited with other members of the press just outside of the Senate chamber. She had taxied in earlier that morning, careful to get a copy of the receipt for her employer so they could properly compensate her later on. She kept the thin paper slip in a small pocket on the inside of her purse. She had the option of a digital copy, but she preferred hard copies, just in case. There must have been enough other people in the Washington, D.C., area who agreed, since paper copies were still offered.

The prayer was concluded, as seen and heard on the flat screens positioned in the waiting space. Sheridan, a handful of other reporters, ushers, aides, and some security saw the cameras change from the zoomed-in view of the pastor to a wider shot of the front of the chamber, the formally dressed figures all turning to the American flag. They put their hands over their hearts and recited the Pledge of Allegiance. They stood at various places amid empty chairs facing away from the banner, the first row of polished brown desks in their semicircle formation, the blue carpeting with light-hued emblems, the long marble desk at the center, with the wall behind it bearing two pairs of marble columns and the gold-lettered sign "E PLURIBUS UNUM," with a square clock perched above it.

"One Nation, under God, indivisible, with liberty and justice for all," concluded the reciters, removing their hands from their hearts and then moving to their respective seats in the chamber. Sheridan paid only moderate attention for the time, as a few of the senators came forward to offer introductory comments. Two elected officials spoke highly of the pastor who gave the opening prayer, both being from his state. Miscellaneous matters were brought up by other senators.

Sheridan took out her voice recorder, a small circular device that, like so many of its contemporaries, had the ability not only to record verbal communication, but also to transcribe it once attached to a laptop. It had near-total accuracy, minus punctuation. Such a nuanced understanding was still the domain of the natural mind rather than the artificial. Furthermore, her device included vocal fillers, something she always deleted as a professional courtesy. Nevertheless, the system made for a more streamlined process from event to story to publication. In her purse, she also had a strap that she could attach the recorder to and wear on her arm if she was on the move for a story or lacked a space to put it down.

She was seated in one of the plush chairs, legs crossed, purse tucked between her right side and the arm of the furniture. The recorder was placed on top of the flattened bag, the copying of the audio near-perfect due to its connection to a special wireless audio service provided to members of the press. On top of her legs was a pad for jotting notes. Among other things, she was planning out possible questions for Senator Benjamin Pettus of Virginia. Dividing her attention between her notes and one of the screens hung on the wall, she soon noticed that the prominent public figure was about to speak. Sheridan turned her attention to the recorder, pushed a button that ended the initial recording track, and then she pushed another button to begin a new track just as Pettus began to speak.

"Fellow senators, I rise today with a great sense of concern over the direction of our elected body. We are not yet two weeks into the new year, and already, my colleagues on the right are trying to pass legislation that would drastically gut our government's healthcare law," said Senator Pettus, dressed as many of the others in a dark suit, white collared shirt, and bright-colored tie. "The measure headed to the Health, Education, Labor and Pensions Committee is a danger to countless Americans who rely on our current federal regulations to guarantee them life-saving medical coverage . . ."

He was one of the older members, with all-white hair and wrinkles. Nevertheless, his passion and oratory made him seem years younger. Pettus had piercing blue eyes and a slim nose and maintained a respectfully shaped frame, due to his well-documented focus on fitness. Sheridan had covered the debate over the healthcare law in the past, as efforts to repeal it had been going on for the past few years. The movement to remove several of the key provisions was gaining partisan ground. Hence, the increased focus of Pettus and other more liberal members of the Senate on preserving the law.

"And I now yield the floor," concluded Pettus, the camera changing its image from a close-up of the orator to the large front of the chamber. He was still visible in the corner of the shot, walking along the edge of the screen to return to his desk.

Sheridan signed into the Page System. It was a recently installed wireless service that allowed reporters to send their requests for in-person interviews with elected officials directly to their desks. Many, including herself, were amused that it took so many years for the system to be installed. When she first came to Capitol Hill for work during her college years, she remembered still having to handwrite requests and give them to others to give to the senators. Login confirmed, she quickly sent a request to Pettus for her story. Meanwhile, her recorder grabbed the remarks of a conservative member of the upper house, taking issue with the doom-filled rhetoric of "the distinguished gentleman from Virginia."

She felt ready for the assignment. There were some planned questions, and if necessary, she could improvise. A beep came from her smart phone. Sheridan knew the noise; looking at the small rectangular screen only confirmed things. The Page System had alerted her that Pettus was on his way. She put a purse-strap over her shoulder, stopped the recording, took hold of the device and her notepad, and then headed toward the chamber doors. A couple of other senators were leaving the chamber, likewise seeking out and meeting journalists for interviews. Soon enough, Pettus pushed open the door, looking down at a small calculator-looking device that provided him with information on the interviewee and included a profile picture to verify appearances.

"Senator Pettus?" she asked, approaching the elected official. He looked up and smiled, offering his hand to shake.

"You must be Miss Sheridan with *The Kensington Post*," he responded, shaking her hand. The two slowly walked away from the doors to one of the areas with plush chairs. "I often read your publication. Very good reporting."

"Thank you, Senator."

"I understand that you wanted to interview me about the health-care law debate?"

"Correct," replied Sheridan as the two sat in chairs that faced opposite one another. "Just a couple of questions."

"Sure," Pettus replied with openness.

"Of course, this interview is on the record. I assume that is acceptable for you."

"Yes, of course," he said with a politician smile. "Wouldn't be the first time."

Sheridan smirked at the comment as she pushed the button on the circular recording device. The bright light confirmed that the audio was being captured and transcribed. "As you mentioned in your remarks, the repeal bill is going through the HELP Committee today. Do you believe it will pass?"

"Unfortunately, yes," he answered. "The committee is full of right-wing ideologues who want to gut our healthcare protections. I expect it to be a party-line vote, but unfortunately, that means a majority will approve it."

"In addition to your remarks this morning, what other efforts will you be undertaking to work against the bill?"

"Once it passes committee, I plan to hold a press conference with people who have benefitted from the healthcare law to stress that this law helps people. I cannot stress that enough; this law helps people. As a doctor by profession, I strongly recommend it. I also plan to urge people to contact their senators. Let them know that this law saves lives. We need it on the books. A society should be judged by how it looks after its most vulnerable. It would be a blot on our society's record if this law is repealed."

"Apologies in advance," stated Sheridan, "but I must ask. Do you believe that you have enough votes in the Senate to defeat the repeal bill?"

"I hope so," he responded. "I really, really hope so. A lot of lives are on the line with this measure. And with elections later this year, my fellow progressives and I must show the American people that we care about the most vulnerable, even if our friends on the conservative side do not. And so, make no mistake: I will be fighting this repeal bill until it is defeated, just like its earlier incarnations in the past two sessions."

"All right then," said Sheridan, offering her hand. "Thank you for talking with me."

"No problem," he said as he shook her hand. "Any idea when the article will run?"

"By early tomorrow morning at the latest."

"Well, how about you let my press person know," Pettus said as the two walked toward the doors leading to the Senate chamber. "Her contact info is listed on Page."

"All right, will do."

"Thank you and take care," said Pettus before returning to the chamber.

Sheridan turned off her recorder, gathered her things, and headed to the Senate Press Office to write up her story. There, her laptop was waiting, being watched over by a professional acquaintance. Like nearly all similar devices, her laptop's screen was a digital projection that materialized once she pushed a button on the keyboard. It appeared with little delay when the button was pushed. Between her rapid typing and the automatic interview transcription, her story was submitted in less than an hour and published by that afternoon. Meanwhile, Pettus was interviewed by four other reporters over the course of the day. He was a high-demand figure, beloved and respected. Some spoke of having him run for president; for now, he was facing an easy re-election come November.

. . . . . .

The Kensington Post was a combination of online and print media, of written news stories, opinion columns, in-depth pieces, and a video department. The automatic cameras and their accompanying anchors produced interviews of public figures, experts, and ordinary folk, live coverage of assorted events, and in-studio reports. Social media carried the live feed to millions. They had a respectable international bureau, with offices in London, Istanbul, and Beijing. That last one was opened only within the last few years due to democratization advances. There were plans to open a fourth office in Tokyo.

The Kensington Post's headquarters was not an elegant palace of a structure, but rather quite basic. Initially, they did not control the whole of their Northwest D.C. high-rise, sharing the ten-story build-ing with a few other businesses and two nonprofits. However, over the past few decades they bought up the remainder of the units. Four of the stories were for archives, two for the print journalists and their editors, three for the video teams, and a tenth for various purposes, including large group meetings or holiday parties. The floor with the print reporters featured groups of cubicles separated by department.

The wall bordering the outside world was glass with black frames. It overlooked a forest of buildings. No clear view of the Washington Monument from their many floors. The opposite wall was also trans-parent, but it was obscured by the interior walls of the editors' offices. A third wall featured four large, flat computer screens that were con-stantly turned to news website feeds. Unlike the screens connected to laptops and office computers, these were solid objects and thus a bit old-fashioned. All but one of the screens was muted. A wireless system changed which screen was un-muted every hour. During an eight-hour shift, each screen was un-muted for two non-consecutive hours. The final wall was the entrance, which was several feet behind another transparent wall that bordered the outside world. It was also comprised of glass. This wall halted before a hallway that had an ex-ternal wall of glass on the other side.

Sheridan was in the Politics Department. As the main office was based in a major city devoted to said industry, that department was quite sizable. There were a dozen full-time reporters, plus another half-dozen or so freelancers and part-timers. Some did quick write-ups on new policy initiatives, often centering on breaking news of introduced legislation, Supreme Court decisions, or sudden resignations. Others went to Capitol Hill or covered rallies, getting soundbites from public figures. Still others did in-depth pieces, getting multiple interviews, expert opinions, and writing up stories that far exceeded fifteen hundred words. Investigative pieces also occasionally ran in this category.

Roberta Sheridan had done them all, one of the few journalists on staff who could basically do anything assigned to her. This was due partly to internships and freelance positions with other publications and partly to her years of experience at the *Post*. By the time she graduated from college, she already had two years' worth of reporting experience, including assignments that took her under the Capitol Dome. She still remembered the nerves in her belly when she first dared to approach a congressman for an interview; now, she did it without a second of fretting.

It was the morning after her interview with Senator Pettus. That day, she did two stories on Congress, writing both of them while at the Senate Press Office. Sometimes, the importance of developing stories in the hall of the most powerful legislature in the Free World necessitated her being there more than her District-based apartment or the *Post's* office building combined. For example, she was there during the long debate over the last bill to repeal the healthcare law, arriving around lunch time and staying until late evening, when the repeal was defeated by only a few votes.

"I bet you're relieved Suarez is covering the final vote this time, am I right?" asked Andrew McClellan, a coworker of Sheridan's. He was on his feet, leaning against the corner of the cubicle wall dividing their work spaces. McClellan was a native of Colorado who had moved to the D.C. area twelve years ago for college and then stayed for work. He went back to the Midwest only for major holidays, weddings, and funerals.

"Yeah, definitely," she said with a nod. Roberta was seated at her desk, her laptop plugged in and web pages up. She had swung her black, ergonomic office chair to face her colleague, leaning backwards so that her seat was tilted upward to view his face. "Thing is, I bet I'll have to cover the Remembrance Day ceremony."

"You sure?" asked a perplexed McClellan. "I thought you could get out of that because of conflict of interest."

"I thought so, too, but technically, I don't have a direct connection to the ceremony. I mean, yes, it happens at my church. However, my church doesn't actually sponsor it, so . . . a little confusing."

"Maybe we should ask the folks at the *Courier* the next time we run into them."

"Oh, please," replied Roberta, waving her hand forward as though to swat an invisible bug. "They'll probably tell us not to show up just so they can get an exclusive."

"Yeah, they would do that," he said with a laugh. McClellan would know, as he formerly worked for the rival news publication until a couple of years ago. During that time, McClellan and his wife were expecting their first, and he was looking for a better paying occupation. When the *Post* offered more than the *Courier*, he altered his loyalties. "In fact, I might have done stuff like that back in the day."

"Of course, you would," she deadpanned, amusing McClellan. Before their speculation on questionable behavior could continue, Roberta received an alert on her laptop. Swinging to face the screen, she saw that their editor was messaging both her and McClellan.

Roberta wrote a quick message confirming receipt of the request and explaining that they were coming. "She is ready for us now."

"Yes, she is," agreed McClellan as Sheridan got up and the two walked over to the Politics Department editor's office. Both carried digital pads to take down notes. They included special pens meant to jot notes on the screens. Each reporter had one, though some still preferred notebook paper and ink pens. Sometimes, Roberta herself used the more traditional means; she held no real preference.

Jocelyn Lopez kept her office door open. Rarely was the portal shut, and rarely did she look at the entrance. Instead, her eyes balanced their time between two screens on opposite sides of her desk. The center of the desk remained open, so she could conduct business with whomever had arrived. While left of center in her politics, in routine, she had several more conservative tendencies. She used paper and pen for notes, seldom sent text messages, and maintained hard copies of her most important documents. And although her husband was okay with her keeping her maiden name, she demanded to take his surname.

"Go ahead and sit down," she said in a welcoming voice, her eyes still focused on the screen to her left. Roberta and McClellan obliged. There was a collection of silent moments as the reporters waited for their editor to come to a stopping point. "Okay, then. All right." A few definitive taps on the keyboard and the project on the left screen was complete. She had two screens and two keyboards. With the project on the left screen done, she tapped a button on the keyboard below it to make the image disappear. She repeated this action with the right screen when she finished that project. Nothing obscuring her view of the two reporters, Lopez finally looked at them. "Now, then. I already saw your story ideas in the pitches chatroom, and I agree that you should work on them."

The two journalists nodded in agreement and relief. Once in a long while, a reporter would be summoned to the editor's office for a failure to give decent pitches to fill a day of work. When Roberta first came to work at the *Post*, this happened once every week or so. As time passed, she got better at pitching ideas. A year ago, she went into a bit of a slump, but with Lopez's help, she was able to get back into the habit of regularly throwing story ideas that typically garnered approval.

"I brought both of you in here to discuss some major stories I want you to work on this week," the editor explained. "These are important assignments that I expect by the end of the week. This will be especially important for you, Roberta." Roberta nodded, with a growing suspicion that she was going to cover the major gathering after all.

McClellan briefly looked at his fellow reporter, assuming the same. His attention quickly returned to his superior as she called his name. "Now, Andrew, I want you to write an in-depth piece surveying some of the notable primary candidates for Congress. Wacky ones, famous ones, feel-good ones. Look for anyone interesting."

"Okay, boss," began McClellan, who jotted down the assignment on his pad, asking a question as his gaze was still downward. "And how many candidates do you want me to include?"

"Shoot for ten for now. If you find only seven really interesting people, then go ahead and do just seven. However, if you can do ten, try."

"Got it," he said as he completed his notes.

"Okay, then. Between that and your current workload, that should keep you busy."

"Yes," affirmed McClellan.

"Roberta?"

"Yes, ma'am?"

"I'm going to need you to cover the Remembrance Day service next Monday."

Roberta felt antsy at the assignment. She shifted in her seat before responding to her editor. "Um, are you sure I can cover it? I mean, the event takes place at my church. I know my church doesn't oversee it, but my pastor will make an appearance. And I know, for a fact, that he is scheduled to speak this year."

"Normally, I would have someone else cover it, but things are getting stretched. Besides, I do not believe there is an ethical conflict here."

"Are you sure?"

"Of course, I am, Roberta," replied a bemused Lopez. "This is a big event with a lot of sponsors. You are not personally profiting from the occasion, nor did you personally fund the event. Your connections are indirect. No professional journalistic society would revoke your credentials over you covering the event."

"Well, if you say so, ma'am, then I will do it."

"Good," said the editor. "As you may know, Remembrance Day turns forty this year. That is a milestone year. Now then, I know that every year, the service brings in a lot of important people. Senators, the president, et cetera. However, being the big four-o, look out for even bigger things."

"Okay, bigger things." Roberta nodded as she quickly wrote her notes. "Do you want me to try and get some interviews?"

"Given how strict the security will be, no need," assured the editor. "And we will use the photos that the White House Press Office posts online and sends via email. Just describe the event, glean some interesting quotes from the speeches, the usual."

"Yes, ma'am."

"In fact, I believe Senator Pettus will be speaking."

"He might have a good word to say," said Roberta.

"Or a good, juicy, provocative comment," interjected McClellan, with a hint of envy. Such over-the-top rhetoric was known to help boost page views, greatly aiding reporters like Roberta in meeting their online hit quota.

"Oh, come on, Andy, do you really think he'll say something inflammatory during the ceremony? Usually such behavior is frowned upon."

"I bet he'll say a whole lot of stuff when the healthcare law gets repealed."

"If," stressed Roberta. "*If* it gets repealed."

"Regardless," stated the editor, taking control of the conversation. "Keep a good ear out for some interesting comments. However, if it is usual solemn remarks and lofty declarations, we can still make a lede with that."

"Yes, ma'am."

"Anyway, you have your assignments. Now carry on."

. . . . . .

Senator Benjamin Pettus was nervous. The efforts to repeal the healthcare law had never gotten this far before. As a member of the upper house who counted his time in office by increments of decade, he had seen the pro-repeal caucus grow over the past several years. Their attempts to undo his work had gotten stronger and stronger. Each congressional election brought in more folk opposed to the healthcare law. At first, the repeal bills never made it past committee. Then they started to get votes in the houses but did not come close to a majority. A few years ago, right after a new Congress was sworn in, the bill narrowly failed in the House of Representatives.

However, this latest attempt went through committee, made it to the House floor, and to the surprise of many, more than secured passage. From there it went to the Senate, again surviving its committee, and was up for serious debate in Pettus' chamber. Only a few of his colleagues were unknown on their views of the repeal bill. Pettus knew that at least forty-five of the senators supported the repeal bill. More frightening, the current administration expressed support for repeal, with the president of the Senate on the record saying that she would break any tie over the bill.

"Year after year, we have seen this federal hijacking of the healthcare system play havoc with the American people," declared a conservative Southern senator, who had voted in favor of every repeal bill that was brought up in the past. "And I, for one, am sick of this happening. This socialized medicine has harmed every country that has tried it. And we are no exception. We must pass this repeal bill. The sooner this failed experiment in Marxist healthcare is gone, the sooner the American people will do better. And I yield the floor."

"Your turn," said Pettus to his friend and colleague Senator Anwar Muhammed. Despite the ethnic and religious differences, the two shared similar political views. Muhammed was twenty years younger than Pettus and owned a pizza business before going into politics. Selling the profitable company gave him the necessary funds to launch a successful campaign to represent New Jersey in the upper house. Like his friend, Muhammed was up for re-election in November. Unlike his friend, his seat was considered a toss-up.

"Inshallah," he whispered back, knowing that if the right people heard the comment, the conspiracy sites would run amok with inflammatory posts. Muhammed was born and raised in Paterson, which was one of over a dozen cities in the nation with a Muslim-majority population. As a result, he spoke both fluent Arabic and English. He was also in the process of learning Spanish to increase his outreach among Latino voters.

Muhammed took a deep breath to get up and approach the microphone to speak against the bill. Recognized as "the gentleman from New Jersey," he approached the floor, briefly looking up at the gallery—that upper space where people came from all over the nation and the nations abroad to behold the legislative process. There was one section allotted to the press, those more interested in getting the closest view of the Senate debate. Unlike others, though, he had invited a specific group to the happenings. They all looked back, giving smiles of encouragement and looks of worry.

"Mr. President," Muhammed began, "I come here to urge my colleagues on the right and the left to vote against this repeal bill." With another breath, he continued, "This is not an issue of right and left; it is an issue of right and wrong. A society is judged on how it looks after its most vulnerable. The healthcare law we have looks after the most vulnerable. Plenty of men, women, and children have benefitted from its provisions. Lives have been saved. From my own home state of New Jersey, thousands have been able to get life-saving coverage. In fact, I have just a few of those many here today watching us from above."

That was the signal. Nearly thirty people—all from the Garden State—representing a multicultural array of races and religions, stood from their place in the balcony seating. This rainbow coalition was, to an extent, staged. Muhammed and his aides purposely picked out folks of varied backgrounds to give the semblance of diversity amid unity. Where the cynicism ended was in the fact that all present sincerely wanted the law to remain on the books. Nearly a hundred elected officials looked up to see them. Many quit after a moment or two, either turning back to the speaking senator or looking down. Muhammed gained in confidence at the showing, thankful that he did not accidentally violate the parliamentary rule of addressing his remarks solely to the president of the Senate.

"These are the people who would be harmed should the repeal bill succeed. These are the faces of those who would be the first victims in this partisan effort," insisted Muhammed. "Granted, our federal healthcare law is not perfect. However, if our friends on the right were truly concerned about the issues in the law, they would seek efforts to remedy these few shortcomings rather than eliminate the entire law as a whole. So, I am urging my colleagues to think logically. If you want to fix something, don't destroy it!" He continued to speak for another two minutes before yielding the remainder of his time. Returning to his seat, he was greeted warmly by Pettus.

After a few more senators spoke their arguments, for and against, a motion was made to end debate. It passed. Then came the motion for a roll call vote. It also passed. So the clerk went through the names of the one hundred elected officials alphabetically, looking down at the list and stoically calling out each appellation. Like the elected officials in the grand chamber, he wore a suit and tie. He had a full beard that was reddish brown, and blue eyes, with a wrist watch on his left arm to count his steps.

"Mr. Adams?"

"Aye!" responded the senator.

"Mr. Adams votes aye," affirmed the clerk. "Mrs. al-Sadaf?"

"Nay!"

"Mrs. al-Sadaf votes nay. Mr. Alvarez?"

"Aye!"

"Mr. Alvarez votes aye. Mr. Collinsworth?"

"Aye!"

Pettus was keeping track on a digital notepad with pen on his desk. He had a column for the ayes and a column for the nays. He was reserved, suppressing the angst surrounding the potential defeat. He feared not for his own health and wellbeing. As a United States senator, his medical coverage was thorough. Further, he was a doctor by profession and, thus, if nothing else, was pretty good at diagnosing himself. It was the greater impact of what was so close to happening. Muhammed sat beside him, looking over his shoulder at the tally. Digital scratch marks showed the ayes in the lead.

"Mr. Diaz?"

"Nay!"

"Mr. Diaz votes nay," confirmed the clerk in a formal voice. "Miss Fitzgerald?"

"Nay!"

"Miss Fitzgerald votes nay."

"I think we're catching up," said Muhammed to Pettus.

"I hope so," stated Pettus. "You're almost up."

Muhammed nodded as the clerk called his name. He declared the nay, and it was recorded. Pettus came next, also stating nay emphatically. The clerk calmly affirmed the passionate vote and went on to the next senator. Pettus went back to marking the two columns with the updated vote. He was not the only person doing that. Many were keeping track—in the chamber, the balcony seating, the press room, on social media, in D.C. bureau offices for numerous publications, and in millions of houses and apartments watching the streaming video of the live roll call.

"Mrs. Salvador?"

"Aye."

"Mrs. Salvador votes aye. Miss Spangler?"

"Aye!"

"Miss Spangler votes aye."

As the clerk was nearing the end of the list, a stirring began amid the many. It came independently for different people in different places. For some, it was an annoyance and even a fret. For others, a relief. Still others, outrage. For the political junkies who followed the senators, who knew their hearts and their minds—or at least their voting patterns—the revelation of the result came as an early wind for the forthcoming storm. Muhammed turned to face Pettus, whose expression of stone seriousness was melting into something new. To get his attention, the New Jersey gentleman grabbed his shoulder.

"I think we're about to win," said Pettus as he turned to his friend, a smile deepening his wrinkles and ease. His additional words prompted Muhammed to look at the small screen on the desk, the marks nearing a total of a hundred. "You see, we have only seven left, and four of them I know to be opposed."

"They don't have enough votes," concluded Muhammed, sharing his friend's support as another senator voted against repeal.

"Mrs. Yalinski?"

"Nay!"

"Mrs. Yalinski votes nay. Mr. Zanderson?"

"Nay!" he declared, knowing that with him came the victory.

"Mr. Zanderson votes nay," said the clerk. The vocal utterances paused as the final vote was tallied. More simmering noise from those in the stands, more outbursts happy and angry on social media. "By a vote of fifty-one nays to forty-nine ayes, the bill has failed to pass." Whatever else the clerk said was lost amid cheering and jeering, booing and applause. Soon after, the session was over, with some reporters submitting breaking news stories that were published within minutes of the news, while others sought comments from those who took part in the widely-watched decision.

"I am thankful to God and my fellow senators who saw the need for this law to remain on the books," stated Pettus before a gaggle of recording journalists and automatic cameras. "Untold numbers of people were saved today. It is my hope and prayer that with this ridiculous repeal bill defeated, the Senate can focus on more important things, like the budget, improving an overhaul on antipoverty programs, and other much-needed projects."

"Voters will remember tonight," declared a senator from Texas who cosponsored the repeal bill. He was likewise surrounded by reporters and bloggers seeking his comments. "Voters will remember who supported a better way for healthcare and who stood against it. Come November, there will be change."

. . . . . .

Roberta Sheridan hated the metro. Many folks in the D.C. area did. Generations earlier, the public transportation endeavor was widely praised for its ever-expanding network of rails. For a small fee, a person could avoid the havoc of driving in the crowded District of Columbia and instead cruise to a desired site for work or vacation. A spider web of trains went above and below the ground to get to federal buildings, National Mall, The George Washington University, Arlington National Cemetery, and so much more. Under the ideal conditions, the various lines helped a busy people on the move.

Yet the principle was always beholden to practice. Delays that situated cramped train cars between stops, malfunctions that generated smoke and sparks, schedule-sensitive businessmen being unloaded from an improperly functioning train a few stops before their own, having to wait long minutes before another train came. Poor maintenance and poorly overseen restoration projects added to the issues. While the system worked far better than it had in past decades, it was still able to put in a bad performance once in a while. One of those bad performances made Roberta late for a work assignment, nearly costing her a much-needed interview. Another had made her late for church.

Roberta refused to put her trust in the metro again. She owned a car and simply weathered the traffic conditions of the District of Columbia. Automobile traffic was not great, but at least it was more predictable than the metro. What's more, since she lived in the District itself, rather than in Virginia or Maryland, her commute avoided some of the more brutal congestion typical of the region. When going outside the office for an assignment, she either drove herself or took a taxi.

For the ceremony, she took her own vehicle. It was a five-year-old black sports compact, with a few small dents and several scratches to the paint job. The handful of nicks did not negate the overall performance of the car, which like most automobiles in its day, ran on a renewable fuel source known as "coil." Short for "corn oil," the blend had corn oil and a host of other ingredients that made for a fuel that replaced the fossilized black gold of the past. Water was its only by-product, ending the debate over climate change fears. To be sure, a small percentage of machines still required the antiquarian material, though they were a shrinking number. Some auto companies had abandoned such fuel sources altogether, while at least one company argued its value for nostalgia purposes.

"Trust in the Lord; He will deliver you," she said to herself, having to navigate some close calls with cars going the opposite direction on a narrow road. "Have faith in the Lord, and He will see you through." It was a common mantra she gave during times of concern. The habit emerged when she first moved out on her own and was in her apartment all alone at night with the lights off. Sheridan kept up the tendency ever since. "Trust in the Lord, and He will deliver you. Have faith in the Lord, and He will see you through." She was relieved as the road cleared and no more cars were trying to pass by on the narrow way.

Sheridan slowed the car as she came into view of the security checkpoint. They were set up on all the streets leading to the church, whose massive structure had been visible for some time. It was still technically a cathedral. The Episcopal Diocese of Washington had never officially terminated their ownership of the worship space. This high church heritage was well-reflected by the exterior Gothic style. From above, it looked like a large cross. There were flying buttresses, more than one hundred gargoyles, and over two hundred stained glass windows, three large towers, and a vaulted sanctuary.

Officially known as the Cathedral of Saint Peter and Saint Paul, the imposing structure remained the space used for many important services, including state funerals; the Inaugural Prayer Service, which took place the day after the Inauguration; and other important ceremonies, like the Remembrance Day event Sheridan was assigned to cover. As The Episcopal Church continued to decline in their membership, so did the Cathedral. This became notably problematic when a new series of repairs to the stonework was required. Donations, even from non-believing patrons, were not enough.

Then came a growing non-denominational congregation known as Forever Life D.C. It was a satellite campus that belonged to the Louisville, Kentucky-based Forever Life Church Network. The multisite congregation boasted tens of thousands of worshippers every Saturday, Sunday, and Wednesday at their eight different locations. All but two of these locations were in Kentucky, with one in New York City and the other in the nation's capital. The latter of the two out-of-state sites grew quickly, going from a dozen folks who met at Chinquapin Park Recreation Center in Alexandria, Virginia, to over three thousand within a decade. Roberta joined the church not long after moving to D.C.

Over time, Forever Life D.C. effectively took over the Cathedral. The dwindling Episcopal congregation moved their worship to Sunday afternoons, leaving the traditional morning time slot for the low church services of Forever Life. The donations from the nondenominational megachurch more than paid for the repairs. Rather than look for a space of their own, the pastors of Forever Life struck a new ownership deal with the bishop of the Cathedral. This allowed the building to be preserved and the nondenominational congregation to have a much lower rent compared to other, smaller religious groups that temporarily used the facility when between worship structures.

Roberta parked her car in the designated parking lots for members of the press and other event workers. Upon opening the door, she received a nice, blustery gust of wind. The frigid welcome prompted shivers but she made a quick recovery. She grabbed her purse, a notebook with a pen, and her digital recorder-transcriber. She chose the old-fashioned paper as the electronic model was frowned upon by security. Her progress to the inside of the Cathedral was slowed by the lines of personnel going through the metal detectors that were set up outdoors. Heating units kept the lines and security folk warm, though the occasional surge of cold air created discomfort. Regardless, the system worked, and Roberta passed the tests of the checkpoints, gathering just outside of the building.

A communications associate with the White House showed up, giving introductory remarks to the dozen or so reporters gathered on the lawn outside the main Cathedral entrance. Photos were going to be provided right after the ceremony by the press pool, as would transcriptions of the speeches. While digital voice recorder-transcribers were acceptable, photography of any kind was unacceptable, and any eating or drinking had to be done outside of the building, with a White House person present. Roberta had already eaten, consuming a small early lunch. From there, she and the other reporters from various publications were led by the associate into the narthex, to the sanctuary along the right aisle, and up several steps to the balcony seating reserved for media.

Roberta took a seat, looking down at the main altar and the growing number of attendees filling the vaulted space. As noontime drew nigh, row after row of connected chairs were occupied by an assortment of important figures. Federal and local politicians, clergy, foreign dignitaries, wealthy families and their heirs, with security lined up along the rows as a complement to the pillars. Several staff members took chairs as well, accompanying the people they served.

Roberta saw Senator Benjamin Pettus coming to the front row. He walked down the center aisle with his wife and eldest son, stopping multiple times when prompted by a familiar face or a kind salutation. Many of the very House and Senate members who so viciously lambasted one another over domestic policy days earlier came together as one at the Cathedral. Many were even amicable toward their foes. In a way, the mood was like a funeral. Some laughter here and there, yet a solemn sensibility prevailing. Senator Pettus even shook hands and exchanged kinds words with the two men who had sponsored the repeal bill. She could not hear their exact interaction, but it appeared lighthearted.

Pettus then did as many other prominent officials and went out of his way to interact with a group of elderly individuals taking their seats in the two front rows of the right column of chairs. A few of them were wheelchair-bound; many had walkers or canes. Nearly all had gray hair, with a couple of them feigning youth with professional dye jobs. A supermajority of them were women. They were distinguished by their sashes: rose-colored, seven-inch wide strips that wrapped around their right shoulders and left hips. Among them were the most emotional, for they fought the good fight decades before; and unlike so many of their peers, they lived to see the battle won and the enemy routed.

Roberta jotted her notes as the pipe organ instrumental began. It was the Cathedral's way of alerting the attendees that the ceremony was about to begin. Remembrance Day had events all over the country—at cathedrals, churches, town halls, and military bases. Overseas, smaller observances were made at embassies, consulates, and even private gatherings of ex-patriates. In a land as heterodox as the United States of America, this was one of the few threads of near-universal commonality. There were some still out there who dared to take a dissenting view, yet they could all fit in a single stadium.

"Ladies and gentlemen," began an announcer positioned outside of the vision range of the press in the balcony. "The President and First Lady of the United States." The vice president and her husband were unable to attend the event. Later on, some partisan bloggers and social media accounts would trash them for missing it. Nevertheless, the mood became formal. No laughter, no idle chatter above a whisper. Once the commander-in-chief was standing in the front row, the National Anthem played. Even the reporters, those who were supposed to be dispassionate observers, stood in reverence, and most placed hands on hearts. The song concluded, the president joined the diocesan bishop, the Speaker of the House, and a few local and religious political leaders, including one of Roberta's pastors.

"My fellow Americans," began the president. "I will be brief, for so much has been said in the past two-score years. On Remembrance Day, we call to mind a darker time in our history. A time when the most helpless among us were slaughtered by the millions. A time when even the most prominent of elected officials celebrated this wanton murder. Remembrance Day, as you all know, falls on the anniversary of *Jane Roe et al, Appellants, v. Henry Wade,* or simply *Roe v. Wade.* This year marks the fortieth anniversary of when that decision was overturned. Today marks forty years of January twenty-second coming without abortion as a legal option. Forty years. For two generations, we have come to grips with the fact that for a tragically long period of time in American history, we accepted the unacceptable. For forty years, we have sought to repair and improve a society that finally gave protection to its most vulnerable. It is as much a time of celebration as it is a time of tragedy. And after forty years, we continue to remember the sacrifices of those who struggled against injustice. Some of these valiant individuals are here today, rightly honored for the movement they championed."

The president directed the large audience's attention to the two rows of elderly activists. Cameras filming the event live likewise directed their viewers to the group. They were all sedate in their responses. Some smiles, some head-nodding. Roberta opted to include the shout-out in her article. In keeping with his promise, the president went only another two minutes from there. It was three minutes until noon. The bishop also gave some remarks and then explained the most notable part of the ceremony. The clock struck noon, and the bells gave a brief melody; then they tolled seven times. The only day of the year when the noon hour came with seven chimes. It was one toll for each of the United States Supreme Court Justices who had formed the majority opinion of that universally hated decision.

CHAPTER 2

HE ARRIVED FIRST. WITH THE outside being chilly and wet, he entered the five-story building in Northwest D.C. and went into an elegant hallway with red carpeting, pillars carved into the ivory walls on either side, and a light blue ceiling with lights. Between the carved pillars were four elevators. He walked to the nearest one and pushed a button, immediately summoning a unit to help send him upward. The doors closed just as a trio of friends entered the hallway as he had earlier, folding up their umbrellas and lowering their hoods. There was no obligation to keep the elevator open, as they were still several feet from that part of the first floor and other units were available.

His reflection was a warped bronze with a thin black line cutting through. Despite the distortions, his key features were discernible. The short, black hair, recently colored to eliminate some early grays. A neck with faint age lines, which were obscured by the "low forest" look that he adopted. It was a trend that emerged in some circles in which a man shaved his face, but let the hair on the front of his neck grow. College students in particular were fond of the look—specially football players, for some reason. Another trendy attribute was his collared shirt, with its intentional wrinkling. That trend was not popular with football players. He wore a net-watch, which warned him of emails entering his primary account and allowed him to make short replies. This bit of technology was commonly worn by executives and managers, especially in the white-collar world.

The decision for which floor to enter was chosen quickly. He had traveled to this professional club before. There was a mix of emotions when the box stopped, the doors pulled to opposite sides, and a new hallway became visible. The young man departed the unit and veered right, walking toward the entrance to the club. His friend had told him to wait. However, he was feeling emboldened. The man at the front entrance was not one he recognized and undoubtedly held a mutual ignorance of the unexpected visitor.

Forward to the goal, an audacity moved him into a minor moral victory. That fueled Michael Chan that night, walking with a confident stride to mask the peril of formality he risked. For him, it was like a clandestine mission, an act of benign espionage. If successful, he had no intention of letting anyone within hearing range forget the grand adventure. If unsuccessful, well, he was unsure of the ramifications. Images of boastful coup circulated into his mind as he got closer to the suited employee standing by the glass wall with a glass door. This guardian was positioned a few feet ahead of the treasured site. Unsuspecting, reserved, as frosty as the outdoor air and as staid as the carved columns on either flank.

"Hello, welcome to the Enemy of the People Club. How may I help you?"

"I would like a table for two, please—by the windows, of course," said Michael with brashness. "My guest is going to be here later."

"Very well," replied the suit, his eyes bending down to review the vacancies on a digital screen that was automatically updated every couple of minutes. "Yes, we do have a few tables that fit your request."

"Excellent," said Michael, smiling.

"I just need to know your credentials."

"My credentials?" asked Michael, his grin weakening.

"You are an official member of the Fourth Estate, are you not?"

"Yes, of course."

"Then please give me your credentials."

"Um, sure, of course," he said, taking a breath before making himself robust in his own mind. "I am Michael Chan, founder, editor-in-chief, and senior reporter at Chan Worldwide News. Based in the D.C. area, no less."

"Uh-huh," replied the suited man.

"You haven't heard of us?"

"How about you show me your official press credentials."

"Well, um, the thing is," Michael said haltingly, "I do not have official credentials, because, because, well because my stuff hasn't been processed."

"Mm-hmm."

"But I am very much a journalist—just not an official one."

"Not an official journalist?"

"Yes," he said, gaining some daring. "In fact, what I am is actually a special kind of reporter, a special kind of newsman. Do you know what I am?"

"Nope."

"I am a citizen journalist."

"Uh-huh."

"I'm serious!" Michael insisted. A moment later, a few folks were coming through the glass door. They were in business casual and a little inebriated, but not so much as to be slurring of speech or staggering of walk. They lightly chatted and laughed, amused and informal. One of them was Andrew McClellan, veteran reporter with *The Kensington Post*. He recognized the man trying to trespass.

"Why, hello there, Michael Chan of Chan News Worldwide," he said, with his two friends from other publications following close behind.

"Hi, Andrew," he responded, annoyed. "And by the way, it is Chan Worldwide News, not Chan News Worldwide."

"Of course, how moronic of me," replied McClellan, his two friends mildly amused. He then turned to the man at the front. "Ben, what is Mikey here doing? He isn't harassing you, is he?"

"He wants to get in, but he does not have credentials."

"I shouldn't need them," Michael stated defensively. "I do just as good a work as any of the folks who get into the club."

"I bet you do," stated a skeptical McClellan. "Tell me, Mikey, since my friends don't know about you, what do you call yourself again? You know, since you're not a professional journalist?"

The comment was biting, but Michael stood his ground. He refused to be shamed by the title he gave himself. "I am a citizen journalist."

McClellan's friends tried and failed to suppress their laughter. McClellan soon joined. Each patted another's shoulder, eyes closed, and one of them even turned a dark pink for want of oxygen. Michael stood there, arms folded. Only the front man conveyed an indifferent mood. Catching his breath, McClellan still had a hand on a shoulder of one of his buddies as he spoke up: "Well, you should all be sooooo amazed, for the 'citizen journalist' has graced us with his wonderful presence."

"A minor miracle," replied the friend.

"The 'citizen journalist' doing some 'citizen journaling.'"

"Yeah, right."

Michael stood firm. "You look here, you so-called professionals. You will not shame me into abandoning my title. I find the stories you're too afraid to cover. I get ledes you would only dream of. People talk to me when they don't trust you. So, yes, I am a citizen journalist, and I hold that above anything else."

There was a pause, a seeming sobering up of the slightly loosened folk between Michael and the glassy entrance. There seemed to be a breakthrough, a possible realization among the doubters that the media figure before them added great value to the world of news. Perchance, there was some respect, some grudging amiability under the mockery. McClellan may have felt it, though he hid it well. The professional reporter turned his back to Michael. He dramatically raised his arms and looked around. A finger pointed upward, pressing against his lips, tapping them a few times while a hand cupped beside an ear.

"Quiet," he said in mocking whisper to his two friends. "Do you hear that?" They shook their heads, still amused, though slightly perplexed at what their acquaintance was insinuating. "The birds have stopped their chirping; the bees are no longer buzzing. The winds and waves have calmed down, and why?" They shook their heads, before hearing McClellan's grandiose sardonic voice boom before them. "Because we are in the presence of a CITIZEN JOURNALIST!" They all laughed with hysteria while an unimpressed Michael kept his arms folded. Their jovial moods seemed to sway them onward, as they finally got to walking past Michael, McClellan giving a minor, older-brotherly punch to the arm.

"No credentials, no entry," stated the suited man. "Unless you are the guest of a member. Sorry."

"Yeah, yeah, I know," Michael replied. "It was worth a try, I guess."

"Uh-huh."

"You were supposed to wait for me," said a woman behind Michael, prompting him to turn around and see the familiar person. She was wearing her usual work attire for the cold months: tight, dark-shaded pants; a button-up blouse of some color; and a light jacket, with flats for better walking and less long-term damage to her posture. Her purse was slung over her left shoulder while her right hand gripped an umbrella. A dark blue lanyard with her press pass attached hung around her neck. She was an attractive adult, with a medium frame; dark eyes; thick, black hair that hit just at the shoulder blades; and light brown skin, the product of her diverse parents.

"Berta!" Michael declared with happiness. "Glad you could make it. I was afraid you would get held up at work. How was work?"

"You tried to go in again, didn't you, Mike?"

"Well, I . . . " Michael started, but then saw that her gaze proved her advanced knowledge. He sighed. "I thought I stood a chance this time." Michael pointed to the suit. "He is new, after all."

"New, but well-informed," the suited man chimed in, eliciting a smile from Michael's female friend. "And no need for you to show me your credentials, Miss Sheridan. I never forget a pretty face."

"Oh, Ben, you're too much," she said, walking by Michael, who elected to walk beside her, back to where the suited man was stationed. Despite the statement, she took hold of her pass and showed it to him. "You know I like to follow the rules."

"Mm-hmm," he replied. "Your usual seating?"

"Yes, for Sheridan and guest by the windows."

"As I was explaining to your guest, we have those available." He handed Roberta a two-inch by two-inch square device. "The chip will guide you to the open spot." The small square showed a bright green arrow that moved like a compass needle.

"Thank you, Ben."

"Yeah, Ben," said a defeated but contented Michael as he walked past the de facto guardian and held the door for Roberta the member.

. . . . . .

An upscale restaurant, the Gridlock Bar and Grill was frequented by many members of Congress. It was a new dining venue, situated between the White House and the Capitol. Utensils were placed in specific formation at each table, all the booths required reservations, and a few back rooms were available for private meetings, usually involving the feasting and dealing of those involved with the powerful. For many visitors, though, there was less politics and more socializing among friends who shared the burden of elected office, being aides to public figures, or holding membership in the much-villainized "Deep State." Some who worked in that world saw this as a safe space of sorts.

Befitting its title, the Gridlock had businesses attached to either of its sides, leaving one wall that led to an alleyway and another that faced Pennsylvania Avenue. The former was there for trash and recycling, the path poorly lit and seldom trod in the eventide hours. The latter was much more presentable, as it was supposed to be. Gridlock's front featured a wall comprised of large, glass squares divided by smooth, concrete beams. An awning protected the main entrance, which was a wide revolving door. Glooming, yellow chandeliers were suspended well above the patrons and waiters.

Senators Benjamin Pettus and Anwar Muhammed were eating dinner at one of the booths. Benjamin had already had a couple of bronze-hued drinks while Anwar contented himself with soda. The Gridlock fancied itself a bit old-fashioned, with orders taken by human waiters rather than the small machines placed at the tables of nearly every other eatery. They also had human cooks do more than just monitor automatized devices. It took slightly longer and involved a little more variance in the end result, but some folks insisted that it made the food taste better and was healthier than modern technology.

"Will that be all, sir?" asked the waitress, wearing a crisp white shirt, dark blue ascot, and black business pants.

"I think I will have a refill," said Benjamin, holding up his beer glass, which had only the dregs remaining, along with a fair amount of foamy residue. The waitress nodded and turned to Anwar.

"Same here," he said.

"All right, I'll be back with your refills," she said before darting off toward the bar.

"I did not realize you were such a drinker," observed Anwar.

"I wasn't at first, but I guess this job is finally getting to me."

"Or you have to celebrate," countered Anwar. "After all, we won."

"Just barely."

"A win is a win."

"So, did your constituents enjoy the tour?"

"Oh, yes, they love this place," Anwar responded. "I took them to the popular sites. You know, the Washington Monument, Lincoln Memorial, Jefferson Memorial. The usual."

"How about museums? We have a bunch of those, also."

"Yeah, they went to the really popular ones. African-American Museum, the aviation one, Museum of the Bible, and, of course, the McCorvey Museum."

"Of course. Especially with the milestone and all."

"Half-priced tickets, so not bad."

Benjamin laughed. "Yeah, not bad at all." The waitress came back with the two new drinks, distributing them to the patrons seated before her. "Thank you."

She nodded. "No problem, Senator Pettus. If you need anything else, I will be back later."

"Sure thing," replied Benjamin as she left. Then turning his attention to Anwar, he continued, "And now we can even toast to the remark." Benjamin gripped his fresh beer, while Anwar took hold of his soda. "To half-priced tickets and miraculous legislative victories."

"Here, here," said Anwar as the two glasses were lifted and then gently touched. Both drank their respective orders for a few moments before continuing. "By the way, did you hear the controversy coming out of my neighborhood?"

"No, what?"

"There's a big push by some local folks to get Barack Obama Elementary School renamed."

"Really?"

"Yes, really."

"Is Grant behind this?"

"How did you know?"

"Grant is usually behind it," said Benjamin as he leaned back and then let loose of his beer, whose cool base was already on the table. "It seems like all she does is go across the country and try and erase history."

"Well, I don't know. I don't really have an opinion on her plans."

"Oh, come on, Anwar," insisted Benjamin. "You're a politician. You have to have an opinion on everything. It was in the job application; don't you remember?"

"Ha," he stated. "Well, right now, I am holding off."

"Discernment, huh?"

"Well, the thing is—"

"Hold on," said Benjamin with a hand raised. His gaze went past his acquaintance and toward the entrance. He was just able to make out the figure of a man he knew. The figure was in his middle thirties, energetic, with dirty blond hair and a glimmer in his eye. He sported a low forest beard. He was inclined to smile and talked it up with a few folks on his way toward the booths. "And he is even coming this direction. Just typical."

"Who?" asked Anwar, who pushed himself a little out of the booth and turned his torso to better view the individual. "Oh, him."

"Yes, him," Benjamin said to Anwar before Johnnie Bedford got closer. His tone became more sociable and boisterous, if not a little patronizing when the newcomer saw him. "Bedford! A pleasure to see you here tonight."

"Greetings, Senator Pettus. And an unexpected pleasure, also," said Johnnie, who came to stand before the booth, his fingers lightly tapping the mahogany table. "Indeed, who would have thought that you would be here?"

"Oh, really?" Benjamin replied in feigned surprise. "You mean, elected officials do not go to a place like the Gridlock? I must be so embarrassed."

Johnnie gave a wry smile. "I was thinking more about that recent vote against repeal. I heard a lot of folks who said nay have been making themselves scarce. Some fear of retaliation or something."

"Or something? Why, Bedford, you're not here to do us in, are you?"

Johnnie laughed. "Oh, no, no, Pettus. Perish the thought. I think you all put up quite a nice fight. I myself was nearly moved to change my mind and start lobbying for your side."

"Nearly, huh?"

"Nearly."

"Correct me if I am wrong, which I know you like to do," said Benjamin, getting a nod of approval from Johnnie. "But I always assumed that it was the losers who hid and ran when the big vote came down."

"Oh, don't you worry, Senator," he replied calmly. "That will happen soon enough. This is an election year, after all. And my peers and connections are emboldened."

"Emboldened, you say? That sounds like a big deal."

"Well, laugh at it as you may, but do not forget what has been happening. The trend is clearly going the other way. It's not too late for you to change your mind. In fact, a fellow with your pull and popularity, I bet you seeing the light would end the debate right there and then."

"Now, now, my pugnacious young friend," lightly warned Benjamin. "If we simply start ending debates, we might as well end liberty itself."

"And what bizarre mind came up with that idea?"

"Actually, you said that to me about a decade ago when it was your side that was losing."

Johnnie nodded at the point. "Perhaps I did." He then turned to see the other person in the booth. "Senator Muhammed, correct?"

"Yes, that's correct," he said with apprehension.

"We haven't met in person before, have we? I am your friend's worst nightmare."

Benjamin laughed. "In your dreams, of course."

"A pleasure, I guess." The two shook hands.

"Well, anyway," Johnnie began as he looked back at Benjamin. "I need to be meeting a party in the back. A bunch of donors are there who are just waiting to fill a war chest or two. Or three. Take care, Senator Pettus."

"You also, my worst nightmare."

"Senator Muhammed," he said with a nod, getting a nod in return just before he returned to his journey to the back.

"I will never get that."

"Get what?"

"How you can make friends with so many right-wingers."

"When it comes down to it, they're decent people. Misguided on a few points, but instilled with a sincere view that what they are doing will help Americans of all backgrounds."

"I guess."

"Besides, we are one fraternal group. We have all been through the same garbage just to get this far in life. Similar personal attacks, similar appeals, similar unrealistic standards. If you think about it, I bet you and I have more in common with Bedford and his Senate friends than we do with most of our own constituents."

"Now I *know* you have had too much to drink," said Anwar, getting a laugh out of Benjamin, who toasted him in response.

. . . . . .

As the two senators were dining at the Gridlock, Roberta Sheridan and Michael Chan were figuring out what they wanted at the Enemy of the People Club. Their selection was not as rich nor as extensive as the Gridlock, but that was of little issue for the two friends. Both opted for burgers and fries with sodas. Roberta did the ordering, typing their orders on the touch screen, including specifics like Michael not wanting a pickle and Roberta wanting some barbecue sauce on the side.

"Anything else, Mike?" she asked Michael, who shook his head in the negative. Roberta pushed the submit button and a confirmation message appeared. From there, a clock indicated the estimated time of arrival for their order.

"You know? I have been wanting a burger from this place all week."

"So that must be why you were trying to get in without me."

"If only."

"Mike, you know the rules," she said, her company rolling his eyes. "To gain entry into the club, you have to have official media credentials from a recognized news publication. Yours has not been qualified yet. So until then, I'm your only way in."

"Or if I make nice with McClellan."

"Or if you make nice with McClellan," she repeated in agreement.

"Citizen journalists should be allowed in, though."

"You really want to start this again, don't you?"

"Yes, I do," he insisted. "I take immense pride in continuing the tradition of the citizen journalist. In the past, citizen journalists made major scoops, documented things that the mainstream professionals were unwilling or unable to cover. People turned off by established journalists turned to the citizen journalists to get their stories released."

"That's all fine, Mike, but you are glossing over the less romantic facts about the history of amateur journalists," countered Roberta. "Remember that nearly all of them had political agendas, which led them to promote dubious and sometimes outright false claims. Many in the early twenty-first century were little better than conspiracy theorists, promoting absurd allegations that sometimes inspired violence. And even the ones who were more honest in their reporting often fell into pitfalls that professional reporters know to avoid."

"Such as?"

"Such as fairness and impartiality. Professionals know to at least try and get both sides of a contentious story. The amateurs do not bother getting the other side, whatever that *other side* may be. Independence of special interests, fully disclosing biases or close ties, avoiding certain assignments due to conflicts of interests—important fundamentals like that. I have seen some of the story posts on your news site, and I can say many of them would never pass muster in a professional reporting environment."

"There are times when mainstream reporters fail those ethics and publish stories very short from telling the truth," countered Michael in the manner in which he sounded like he had already won.

"Yes, there are the occasional flaws, the occasional mistakes," began Roberta. "However, there is also accountability. The reason you know these mistakes occurred is because professional news media issue corrections, disciplines or fires offenders, and so forth. When was the last time Chan Worldwide News issued a correction?"

"You mean, we can't just change the online print?"

"Point is, Mike, there are rules. Standards. When your publication starts adhering to the rules, then you will probably get that approval from the journalism community."

"You know something, Berta," said Michael, being one of a small number of people among the living allowed to call her that, "you might have a point. A good reshaping of Chan Worldwide News might just be in order."

"If you have any questions, I can do my best to answer."

"And in return, the next time I have a big story, I will let you in on it."

"Unlike the small stories you feed me from time to time, right?"

"Right," he agreed. "When I find a big one, I will contact you, and we can do a joint feature on it. That way, we both get credit."

"Joint feature? Mike, *The Kensington Post* does not cross-promote news articles. Opinion columns, yes, but not news stories."

"But you can still give me partial credit . . . you have done it before."

"You mean the 'Michael Chan of Chan Worldwide News contributed to this report' line at the bottom of my stories that you helped with?"

"Yeah, that," said Michael with a nod. "My news site always sees a bump in hits when that happens. And if you write a really big story and give me partial credit, that will really help my news publication make it to the big time."

"Okay, I can do that," said Roberta. "Whatever helps to feed the beast that is my good friend's life's work." Just then, a box-shaped robot with wheels rolled up to them. It was the same height as their table. Once its rectangular top was parallel to the table, the top opened and two fresh, warm orders were raised upward for the club member and her guest to grab.

"Speaking of feeding . . . " remarked Michael as the two took their respective orders from the elevated platform. Once the plates were removed, the small platform lowered back into the box. The top closed, and it rolled back toward the kitchen, censors alerting it to any pedestrian getting in its way. Michael was about to speak, but he kept quiet as Roberta bowed her head and gave a brief silent grace. As she looked up again, Michael spoke: "I am serious, Berta. If I hear about a big story, one that would be like a 'story of the century,' I promise to let you in on it. Something that explosive might require an expert."

"Got it," she said as she removed the top bun and poured the barbecue sauce onto the lettuce and tomato that covered the beef patty. "And I am only too happy to help you craft a story that's ethics-friendly."

"That might actually work," he quipped just before taking his first bite into his dinner.

. . . . . .

There were more people than usual at Sunday morning's worship service. Roberta was pretty familiar with the regulars, knowing most either by face or by name. She was part of a small group, which did classes before the worship service and occasionally gathered during the week for social events. The different people at that morning's service skewed older than the ones with whom she was familiar. Roberta knew the reason for their presence as they were part of the National Cathedral's congregation. She rarely encountered these people during the week, as their service came hours after her church worship had concluded. In an ordinary week, the two did not mingle.

However, once in a long while, usually three to four times a year, the two congregations that shared the Cathedral worshipped as one in the Body of Christ. Their service would reflect this fusion, with more high church attributes as part of the order of worship. Roberta was born and raised an evangelical, so things like an alter processional, liturgy, and many of the older hymns were exotic to her. Nevertheless, as a nondenominational believer, she was open to periodically experiencing such aspects. They did her no harm, after all. In her opinion, it seemed as though the greater adaptation struggle came for the Episcopal contingency. Perchance, that was one reason why they were disappearing.

"You may be seated," said her pastor, who wore jeans and a purposely wrinkled long-sleeved plaid shirt, sharing the front of the sanctuary with a trio of clergy who wore flowing garments and Roman collars. The contemporary evangelical leader shook hands with the bishop, who then ascended the ornately carved pulpit that Roberta never saw any of her pastors use when delivering a message.

"Our lectionary reading for today comes from the Old Testament book of Nehemiah, chapter eight, verses one through three, five through six, and eight through ten." The bishop read the sacred text, which spoke of the Israelite exiles returning from the Babylonian Captivity. It spoke of the Prophet Ezra coming before the people and reading the Law of Moses, a moment that brought the multitudes to tears.

> And Nehemiah, which is the Tirshatha, and Ezra the priest the scribe, and the Levites that taught the people, said unto all the people, This day is holy unto the Lord your God; mourn not, nor weep. For all the people wept, when they

heard the words of the law. Then he said unto them, Go your way, eat the fat, and drink the sweet, and send portions unto them for whom nothing is prepared: for this day is holy unto our Lord: neither be ye sorry; for the joy of the Lord is your strength.

Roberta listened reverently as the guest clergyman gave his homily. To his right, the altar bore the elements of Holy Communion. The table was open to all believers, so neither Roberta nor her peers had to worry about being excluded. As expected, the bishop gave a sermon centered on the anniversary of the Roe v. Wade decision. As the people wept when hearing the Law read, he explained, so he hoped those gathered will weep internally when hearing about their former culpability in the abortion industry. The bishop admitted, at times in a great emotional state, the former support for abortion that far too many of his spiritual ancestors held onto with earnest. How Episcopal clergy were known to actively campaign against laws abolishing the practice, how a few ordained souls went as far as to bless with holy water abortion clinics, sanctifying the procedure.

"It is a distressing thing to remember, my Church's former love for the unlovable, abominable, pagan-like practice of abortion. The many laity and clergy who dedicated their lives to funding and performing these things are a mark of great sadness. I myself have longed to reach out, to confess, and to seek forgiveness for our sins, both of action and inaction. We cannot change what happened, but that is no excuse to not observe it, to weep at the sound of these written facts being spoken. Even we frozen, chosen Episcopalians are capable of deep emotional contemplation over our former transgressions."

The self-deprecating comment brought some smirks and brief giggles from the audience, mostly those who worshipped with the very reverend figure on a weekly basis. In past years, when covering the various observances connected to Remembrance Day, Roberta recalled a few stories about churches and political groups issuing official apologies for once supporting the practice of terminating in-utero life. A few took the recanting beyond words, joining demonstrations and petition drives to get the names of certain schools and streets changed, as well as statues removed.

For Roberta, her faith and her profession complimented each other. As a youth, she had a pastor who emphasized the need for the faithful to be witnesses in secular realms. The preacher had bemoaned the false assumption that one was only required to advance the Gospel as a clergyman and that church administration work was the only sacred work. She took it seriously, the belief that Christian faith could positively direct the methods and objectives of secular careers. She fused in her mind the biblical principles of truth, honesty, showing partiality to none, and personal discipline and accountability to a profession that historically has been more non-religious than the general population. Roberta took comfort in this harmonization, rejoicing that even she could serve God as a journalist. This also meant that she took it all very seriously, especially the standards for her occupation.

With the sermon concluded, the two congregations joined as one to recite the traditional Apostles' Creed. Some of the folks around Roberta were able to speak it from memory; she had to look at the screens hoisted on either side of the gathered souls. Soon enough, the Episcopal clergy helping to lead the service presided over communion. Again, the screens were necessary for the vast majority of the attendees, due to their association with the more informal weekly worship of Forever Life D.C. It was one of the few times that Roberta heard the massive pipe organ in a service, used for the musical portions and played as the rows of attendees rose and filed into two straight lines going down the center aisle of the sanctuary. Roberta, like the others, received the sacrament.

Her congregation regained the central focus following the sacrament, with the praise band leading the two groups of Christians into a contemporary worship song. Some of those belonging to Forever Life raised their hands and swayed to the music; the Episcopalians remained still and focused on singing the lyrics. A rector gave the closing benediction, and the service was concluded. There was a good deal of socializing as people made their way toward the main exit. Roberta turned her phone on as she left the Cathedral and entered a warming winter day, where small enclaves of snow remained on grassy spaces. Her device alerted to a message she received while at worship: "Hey Berta! I FINALLY got the big story. We need to meet up tomorrow after work. You WON'T be sorry!"

CHAPTER 3

ROBERTA SHERIDAN WAS JUST A girl when the Norma McCorvey Memorial Museum was officially opened. Her parents took her to the ribbon-cutting ceremony, traveling both ways on crowded metro trains, for they had lived in Northern Virginia at the time, her mother pregnant with Roberta's little sister. Tens of thousands attended; the president and vice president both gave speeches, as did the mayor of the District of Columbia. They scheduled the occasion on the anniversary of when the 1973 decision had been overturned, so to the surprise of few, the weather was hot and humid.

By contrast, the adult Roberta waited outside of the McCorvey Museum with a thick jacket on and a scarf around her neck and head. Her breath was visible and her hands were gloved. The sun was still out, though it was fading. Once Roberta completed her work for the day, she was allowed to leave the office early. Her editor assured her that if anything sudden came up, a colleague would write up the piece. Even if they required her presence, the museum was within walking distance of her office.

Michael Chan had texted her to come to the museum. She pressed him for more information about his "big story," yet she got nothing specific. There were times when this habit of Michael's to withhold excitable news got on her nerves. Given her several minutes of waiting in the frigid outdoors, this was one example. She paced back and forth, with the museum about thirty feet away. There were other people doing likewise, waiting for friends or family. One was looking down and texting feverishly, albeit with a stoic countenance. Another was leaning against one of the two waist-level stone walls on either side of the main entrance of the building. Roberta considered such a positioning odd, for the wall had to be hard and cold. At least, she only had to deal with one of those issues.

"You made it!" declared Michael, speedily walking toward his friend.

"I texted you that I was here," she reminded him.

"Oh, I didn't notice."

"And you wonder why you're still single."

"Takes one to know one, right?" he said with a smile as the two hugged briefly. They turned to face the pillared front of the museum. There were nine columns, each with the twin symbolism of a month of gestation and a member of the United States Supreme Court. "You ready to go inside?"

"What do you think?" she incredulously declared.

"Then in we go," agreed Michael, taking out a card and holding it with one of his gloved hands. "And I will be a gentleman."

"Thank you."

Roberta and Michael walked toward the Museum entrance, crossing into the towering structure's expansive shadow. The building was partially modeled off of the Thomas Jefferson Memorial, with long stairs that went up to a domed edifice. The large semisphere ceiling represented the womb. Above the four pairs of double doors was included a statement by the third president of the United States, which the designers of the McCorvey Museum believed was fitting for the narrative:

I am not an advocate for frequent changes in laws and constitutions, but laws and institutions must go hand in hand with the progress of the human mind. As that becomes more developed, more enlightened, as new discoveries are made, new truths discovered and manners and opinions change, with the change of circumstances, institutions must advance also to keep pace with the times. We might as well require a man to wear still the coat which fitted him when a boy as civilized society to remain ever under the regimen of their barbarous ancestors.

"Good to get inside," stated Roberta, loosening her scarf and placing her gloves in her purse. Before them were three checkpoints with body scanners. Replacing the antiquated combination metal detector and baggage scanner, the two simply walked one at a time through a metal arch and were confirmed as having nothing malevolent on their person. Every so often, as was the custom in other secured facilities, a visitor was chosen at random for a second search, using handheld wands that double-checked the archway's conclusion. As neither Michael nor Roberta were chosen, the two walked into the museum's large, open central room with little delay. "So, where to now?"

"The tour, of course," Michael replied.

"Is this really necessary?" she critically inquired. "You cannot simply tell me what your 'big, huge, awesome story of awesomeness' is?"

"Humor me," he insisted. "After all, I'm paying."

"Like a gentleman."

The two walked in a straight line, as the tour took place in a long, narrow room directly opposite the main entrance. To their immediate left was a gift shop featuring the usual overpriced items, tourist souvenirs, candy, postcards, and other miscellaneous commodities. Beside the shop was a hallway that led to administrative offices. To their right were the public restrooms and a hallway that led to storage for the large volume of historical artifacts and documents related to various themes pertaining to abortion. There was also an alternate walkway to the various historic displays if a visitor did not want to take the tour. Most, however, felt an obligation to see the images and sounds of the past.

"You scared?" Michael asked as he took out a money card.

"Excuse me?"

"I remember when we here back in eighth grade and I got you to take the adult version of the tour with me. You were freaking out!"

"No, I wasn't," replied Roberta, defensively. Michael looked at her with disbelief. "I cried some, yes. But I mean, who wouldn't?"

"I'm not judging, Berta. I am just making sure you are okay with taking the adult tour again."

"Mike," she stated. "I am twice as old as I was back then. I will be just fine."

"Challenge accepted," he said as he tapped his card on the monitor in front of the tour room's entrance two times, bringing forth a pair of tickets. He handed one to Roberta, who said a fleeting thank you in response. They were joined by a handful of others. Not a large crowd, but on a Monday afternoon, such was not expected. Two uniformed human beings stood on either side of the room's entrance, scanning tickets. They had stools behind them should they grow weary. From there, the hallway split into two sets of doors, one for the adult tour and the other for the student tour. On the archway above the adult tour was a warning for attendees about the graphic nature of the audiovisual content. A windowless journey into a darkened room. For those coming, it felt like a movie theater.

All the people stood up in the dark room on a black-colored moving walkway, not unlike the ones found at airports. On either side of the guests were large screens that would show the same images once activated. At that point, as the tour was still pending, each screen showed a clock counting down until the beginning. Small conversations were taking place among the varied folks waiting for the tour to begin. The clock was winding down. Michael looked at Roberta to make sure she was okay. She expressed with a glare her annoyance at his worry. They remained side-by-side as the clock went down to zero.

The screen that the two were watching went totally black. Then a long note from a violin was heard. A couple of other stringed instruments joined in. A collage of images began to appear on the screen. They included a sonogram, waves of protesters, and photos of past Supreme Court justices, politicians, and infamous abortionists. A loud deep narrator voice garnered the attentions of all and surprised a few of those paying attention to one of the two screens. "In the history of the United States of America, there are many days of infamy. April 15, 1865. October 29, 1929. December 7, 1941 . . ." The dates popped up on the screen in bright thick lettering to contrast with the darkened imagery. ". . . September 11, 2001. And yet, no day of infamy has claimed more human lives and harmed America more than January 22, 1973." That last date loomed in the largest print. "You will now go on a journey through the struggle to recognize that all life should be protected by law."

The word "journey" was the cue for the walkway to begin working. A slight jut and the group of standing visitors smoothly ventured forward. Creators of the tour wanted to give guests a sense that they were moving forward in a march through history. Splattered images of the Supreme Court in 1973 and some of the key figures from the litigation, including the namesake of the museum, appeared and faded on the screens. Each included basic written information—names and birth and death dates for those involved. These images reappeared and then faded gradually as the figures were mentioned by the narrator, who continued: "On the day of infamy, January 22, 1973, an all-male Supreme Court ruled seven to two that an in-utero human life could be murdered for any reason. While the *Roe* majority opinion technically allowed for some restrictions on abortion, the lesser-known companion decision of *Doe v. Bolton* opened for a broad interpretation of when an abortion could occur. The result . . . was nothing short of barbarism on a grand scale."

The images turned crueler. Disturbing machine noises filled the room; photos of the inner rooms of abortion clinics were matched by unnerving, purposefully off-key music and high-pitched vocal notes. "Tens of millions of lives were exterminated in clinics not unlike these. From the day of infamy and into the birth of the twenty-first century, more helpless human beings were killed by the American abortionist than by any other cause of death. Even the tragic losses incurred by the AIDS virus were dwarfed by the many unborn who were disposed of because they were labeled 'choices.'"

From there, the narrator began to show the most gruesome of the images. Some were undercover videos taken by activists from the time. Others were dramatic reenactments based off of the recollections of former practitioners. The blood and the body parts, the callous discarding of infant corpses into trash bags. Macabre experiments on the pieces of what was once living. Roberta gripped Michael's left hand in her horror. Michael looked at her, and she looked at her clasping hand. She let go of her grip upon looking at Michael's face and then folded her arms before returning to the screen, whose images moved on to other displays.

"Some may wonder how such blatant atrocities were allowed to exist for so long. The answer was that in those days, politicians, media, celebrities, and well-funded lobbyists were able to marginalize the concerns of many who spoke against the genocide."

The narrator paused his comments and the screens showed old footage of notable public figures speaking on the issue of abortion. Some of the guests were surprised to learn that the first African-American president of the United States and the first woman to win the popular vote in a presidential election were among the strongest advocates for legalized abortion.

Then the narrator returned. "However, as the famous civil rights activist Dr. Martin Luther King, Jr. stated, the 'arc of the moral universe is long, but it bends toward justice.' As the twenty-first century began, efforts to stop America's worst Holocaust began to make gains. An increasing number of Americans became outraged by an industry built upon the deaths of the most helpless. Legislative efforts, movies, campaigns, and the proto-Remembrance Day observance known as the March for Life, began to sway the public."

"Here comes the important part," whispered Michael to Roberta, causing her to briefly turn to face the speaker before going back to looking at the screen.

"In the twenty-first century, two infamous abortion providers unintentionally swayed many to support the Pro-Life Movement. The first of them was Dr. Kermit Gosnell, the late-term abortion provider known for allowing female patients to die and for murdering babies born alive. Criminal investigators would label Gosnell's Philadelphia, Pennsylvania, clinic a 'House of Horrors.'" The screen showed more graphic images from the former clinic, as well as a portrait of Gosnell and footage of his trial. "The other major figure of growing outrage was Dr. Edgar Billings Hood. A native of Boulder, Colorado, Dr. Hood moved to California to practice abortions. At his nightmarish facility, babies were murdered before and after birth, with Hood engaging in sinister experiments on their remains. For these crimes against humanity in the name of a perverted science, he is forever known as the 'American Mengele.' Soon after California outlawed abortion, Hood would disappear without a trace."

"Was that the important part?" Roberta whispered to Michael. He nodded. Both of them turned back to the screen as the music got more upbeat. The narrator described the final decision and subsequent legislation that led to the striking down of *Roe v. Wade*. Video footage of emotional rallies in support of the decision, of church bells ringing. And then the tone became somber once again. "However, contrary to what many may believe, the fight to end the slaughter was not yet over. Several states denounced the decision and refused to enforce it. This prompted the president to send thousands of National Guard units to compel compliance with the ruling. Violent clashes occurred in several major cities, with the worst taking place in Los Angeles, California; Seattle, Washington; Ithaca, New York; New York City; and the District of Columbia." With each name uttered by the voice, a map of the U.S. had said city engulfed with a great fire. News footage of the time was also included. "A network of illegal abortion practitioners formed, its organizers daring to draw parallels to the Antebellum Era's Underground Railroad.

"Yet, the uprisings eventually cooled. This came in large part because of Congress' passage of a law guaranteeing amnesty for all abortion providers. Additional funding for both private and public charities to provide alternatives to abortion also aided the cause. And the sheer march of time has ended the urge to kill the helpless. As the nation celebrates four decades since the overturning of *Roe v. Wade,* we see the maturing of yet another generation of women and men who would never consider the murder of a baby to be a valid option in times of trouble." A collage of diverse people with an American flag in the background took over the screen. A patriotic instrumental played. "In the history of the United States, we struggle to live by the principles of life, liberty, and the pursuit of happiness. With the end of *Roe,* we as a society have come even closer to that high ideal."

. . . . . .

Roberta and Michael walked out of the tour room. They entered a hallway that had multiple rooms with broad entrances. Each chamber had a theme related to the history of abortion and its abolition. A married couple was to their right, looking at some quotes painted on the wall from leaders of old. "Wow, I can't believe that the American Civil Liberties Union used to be totally pro-abortion."

"Yeah, we should tell your brother," said the husband to his wife. "He'll freak out for sure."

"Well, that was interesting," commented Roberta. "Now, what is the story?"

"You mean, the big story," corrected Michael.

"Okay, Mike, the 'big story.'"

"Just got to show you one more thing."

"Really, Mike?" protested Roberta. "This is getting a little annoying."

"I promise," he assured her. "One more thing. Follow me."

Roberta humored her friend and followed him into one of the chambers. The section had several items pertaining to Dr. Hood, one of the villains of the tour video. The walls featured photos of the man, one of which he gave what looked like a sadistic smile. Another showed him standing proud in front of his clinic. Glass boxes secured historic items from his handiwork. Some of the clamps and blades, a lab coat that still had splotches of dried blood, several small containers where he once held experimented samples of fetal tissue and tiny limbs, and even a broken wristwatch. Michael led Sheridan to a prominent image of Hood, standing with a group of others at a demonstration protesting the then-novel Supreme Court decision striking down the right to an abortion.

"You see him? You see what it says about what happened to him?"

"Same thing as the tour, Mike. He disappeared."

"All right, all right," said Michael, giving a dramatic pause. "Now, what if I told you that I have found Dr. Hood?"

Roberta smirked. "So, where was he this whole time? The Bermuda Triangle? Area 51? Maybe he was touring with Charolash."

"No, no, Berta," Michael said, tapping his phone screen a few times before turning the image so Roberta was able to see it. "He has been in plain sight for years." Roberta saw the photo that Michael presented and was visibly disturbed by her disbelief.

"You have got to be kidding me," she stated. "Mike, are you serious?"

"Very serious."

"Senator Benjamin Pettus?" She shook her head. "You brought me through all this to tell me that the Senator Benjamin Pettus is the 'American Mengele' in disguise? You spend too much time on the internet."

"Oh, come on, Berta, give it some consideration," insisted Michael. A small number of people slowly moved around the room, giving them little attention. "I'm not the first person to accuse him of being an abortionist."

"It's common practice to accuse older liberal politicians of being abortionists. It pretty much happens to them all at one point. Like a rite of passage."

"Still, I'm telling you, you know this has more to it," he said, as the two walked deeper into the display room, ever surrounded by the images and paraphernalia of the nefarious figure and being farther away from the others. "He's basically the same age as Hood and the same height. They both have a medical background. And what's more, there's the chronology. You don't find it suspicious that not long after Hood goes missing, Pettus appears? Remember, we have nothing from Pettus' past other than what he claims."

"Yes, and there is an obvious explanation for that," countered Roberta. "He, along with about fourteen million other Americans, was a victim of the Ultralord Virus. That techo-plague destroyed a lot of evidence for people's backgrounds. Not just his."

"Okay, maybe that's valid."

"And what's more, he looks nothing like Hood. Different eye color, facial structure. Mike, we look more related than they do."

"Okay, okay, all right," said Michael with hands raised, one gripping his phone. "So I don't have all the answers. But I have something no one had before now. Not the past political ads, not you, or anyone else."

"And what would that be?" asked a skeptical Roberta with arms folded.

"A witness."

Roberta's resistance loosened.

"On Remembrance Day, a woman messaged me online claiming to have worked as a nurse at Hood's abortion clinic. We corresponded a little before we set a date to meet in person. Now, at first, I was just as skeptical as you, trust me."

Roberta looked at him with judgment.

"Okay, maybe not that skeptical, but not gullible. I went in with a reserved view. But after I talked with her, heard her story, I've become a believer."

"Maybe I should tell my pastor the good news."

"Seriously, Berta, give her a chance," pleaded Michael, holding up his phone.

"Okay," she said after some hesitation. Roberta took out her phone. She held it up as he tapped it with his mobile device, causing a small amount of data to transfer seamlessly between the two phones.

"Great. Her name is Etna Lee. She will be uber-happy to speak with you."

"I still need to clear this with my editor."

"Of course, but I know your editor is a smart woman. She will not want to avoid this."

"We will see. However, I cannot promise anything."

"I get it, but I am optimistic."

"You always are."

. . . . . .

"The struggle for equality did not begin in the 1960s," stated Senator Benjamin Pettus, as viewed by Roberta Sheridan on a digital screen in an office cubicle. "Resistance to the oppression of slavery, racism, and segregation draws all the way back to the first slaves who refused to bend to their masters. It continued with the marginalized taking up arms to free their brothers and sisters during the Civil War. It was maintained by the pastors who campaigned against a wave of proposed Jim Crow laws following Reconstruction. Resistance against evil is a persistent theme for the African-American community."

Senator Pettus was speaking before a gathering of African-American clergy and lay leaders that afternoon. While most of the schedule involved faith leaders, Pettus was among the small number of political figures, and the only Caucasian. Indeed, he even cracked a joke about the matter earlier. Roberta watched while sipping her coffee, her computer perfectly transcribing his every word. When a statement sounded interesting, she dragged her finger along the words, selecting the preferred text to highlight. Later, when looking over the completed transcript, she would have the key quotes ready.

For the article, she had already typed up some background, both on the convention event that Pettus was attending and on the senator's civil rights record. During his time as a member of the Fairfax County Board of Supervisors, he had championed racial reconciliation efforts as well as improvements on the quality of predominantly black schools and neighborhoods. Several of his staff were people of color and he often visited historic African-American schools and churches when on the campaign trail.

"How's he doing?" interjected Andrew McClellan from behind, prompting Roberta to swing her office chair around to face her coworker.

"Just fine. Nothing scandalous."

"So much for clickbait."

"Not every story about a political figure has to be inflammatory. Sometimes, they just do something good for the world around them."

"But only sometimes," countered McClellan with a smile. Roberta smiled back as she turned back to the screen and highlighted another possible quote for her article. "Anyway, going in to see our luddite editor about my longer term stories. Heaven forbid we do this through instant chat, am I right?"

"Heaven forbid," Roberta repeated, ocular focus on screen. After finishing her coffee, she tapped the screen where the video of Pettus was, instantly grabbing blur-free images to use with her story.

Listening to Pettus, Roberta was beginning to regret agreeing with her friend to pitch a story idea like the one she was pitching. Here was a man of charity and civility, who rarely engaged in personal attack or vicious partisan rhetoric. A man who had been in the public eye for decades and yet nary a scandal had befallen him. He was not a perfect person. As someone who had often covered his career, Sheridan was able to name a few instances here and there when he fronted a poor argument or said something questionable in its content. Yet, by and large, she respected Pettus as a person and as a politician.

"And so, as a way providing more than just kind words and nice speech for your cause, I have decided to make sure that my faith is not without works," Pettus stated. "And so, it is with great pleasure that I come to this godly convention with good Christian charity." Then Pettus took an envelope from his dinner jacket and showed it before his audience. "This is a check for 125,000 dollars to benefit the university, which is sponsoring this convention, and this blessed organization, which does so much for so many." Roberta's eyes widened. The surprise was genuine, as no advance press releases of the speech had mentioned his intention to donate such a large sum to the community.

Roberta dragged her finger along the text, from where he began to speak of his donation all the way down to the proceeding comments. She knew she had her lede. She tapped the video image, securing a photo of Pettus holding the donation up high. From there, she went to a different web page and notified her editor, Jocelyn Lopez, about the development. She gave a quick confirmation that the lede was solid and would be edited as soon as the story was submitted. Background information already written, the instant transcriber having already printed his words, and Roberta's own speed and efficiency, the article was submitted within minutes of the breaking announcement.

As another speaker took to the video feed, Roberta leaned back in her chair with an ease of accomplishment. Minutes after her work was submitted, it was posted at the center of the Politics Department webpage. Soon after that, the social media team carried it on the various sites, further upping the hit count for her work. Looking into the admin page for her articles, she saw that the number of views for the story were quickly rising into the hundreds and then the thousands. Some of her older pieces had failed to get as many hits in days as that story had in less than a half an hour.

"The luddite told me it was your turn," McClellan said as he walked by. "Because of how well your story is doing, I think she is in a good mood."

"Thanks, that should help," said Roberta, getting up from her chair and going toward Lopez's open office door. Sure enough, upon entering the view of her superior, she saw the editor cracking a smile.

"Already up to four thousand," nodded Lopez, a bigger smile emerging. "I bet we scooped *The Courier* really well this time."

"Yes, ma'am."

"Come on and take a seat, Roberta."

She obliged.

"I have gotten down the assignments for McClellan and Suarez. That just leaves you," the editor said while clicking out of screens, the desk cleared of obstruction. She then focused her sole attention on the journalist. "So what do you have?"

Roberta was feeling anxious. There were many doubts about the idea she was going to pitch. The central claim was one that she herself found questionable, if not absurd. Nevertheless, she had told her friend that the story was going to be pitched. She had the contact information for the woman he wanted her to interview. What was more, Roberta lacked any other good story ideas that she could see her editor approving as an in-depth piece. She kept calm, showed no visible signs of this conflict, and responded.

"I have a possible story in mind, one that, if true, could be a major scoop, beating out not just *The Courier,* but all the other news sources."

"Go on, you have my interest."

"You know that my friend Michael Chan has his own news site and that, from time to time, he sends me story ideas," said Roberta. Her superior nodded and showed a clearly dampened optimism. Roberta pushed on despite the visual cue. "Well, he has directed me to a woman who claims to know the current location of Dr. Edgar Hood."

"The 'American Mengele' himself? And where would that be?"

"Well, as of right now, an African-American convention being held at an HBU."

Lopez thought a moment. Sheridan wondered if she had to spell it out, but that turned out to be unnecessary. "Hold on, you're saying that Senator Benjamin Pettus is Dr. Hood in disguise?" The editor said it as though about to laugh.

"I just want to say that I do not believe it either. I told Mike that I thought it was ridiculous. However, he insisted that I speak to this woman. Supposedly, she used to work with him at the West Coast Clinic for Women. With your permission, I can set up an interview with her and get an idea for what her claims are."

Lopez took a breath, lowering her head so that a few of her fingers were supporting her right temple. "You want me to let you interview some random woman who might be totally nuts and give her a platform?"

"That was what I was thinking, but I did a search on her. Her name is Etna Lee, by the way. And when I searched Lee, nothing suspicious came up. No conspiracy theory blogs, no crazy social media posts, no criminal record . . ."

"No history of mental illness?"

"Nothing that made headlines, anyway."

"I see," replied the editor, who returned to a better posture. "I am trying to be fair. When it comes to down to human nature, no one is really beyond anything. When I first started out, I was a crime reporter. Oftentimes the convicted killer was a nice man with a good family who paid his taxes and attended church every Sunday. So, I get that. I am still a little apprehensive with this coming from Chan."

"In Mike's defense, he's never steered us wrong. Every time I have written a story from one of his ideas, it has turned out to be true."

"Usually partially true," commented Lopez. "I still remember that one lawsuit against a group of anti-repeal protesters outside Senator Collingsworth's office. He claimed that the charges were dropped when it turned out it was only true for one of them."

"He was not that far off," countered Roberta. "And besides, I found it out before we went to print. His eye for stories and my eye for critical thinking have produced some good articles. And the only price we paid for it was to give him partial credit at the bottom of the page. Jocelyn, I am confident that, if nothing else, there is a story of some kind here. Even if it is not the one that Mike thinks."

Lopez took a deep breath. "Okay, okay. Go ahead and interview the woman. And if there is something, I will let you pursue this."

"Thanks," said a relieved Roberta as she rose from her chair.

"But just remember, Roberta, that we need to be very careful on this. *The Kensington Post's* reputation will be in great danger if we run something that's wrong. Got it?"

"Yes, ma'am."

. . . . . .

New Hope Pregnancy Care and Resource Center was based in an unassuming office building in Fairfax County, Virginia. It was a simple three-story structure that shared a large parking lot with a few other business buildings. The stretch of manmade pavement and brick-and-mortar lay between two clusters of trees off of Ox Road, a major street that had a broad collection of entities along its sides—among them a country club, a large recreational park, a few houses of worship, shopping centers, gas stations, some wilderness, and the main campus of George Mason University.

Roberta Sheridan drove to the location. It was a contrast from her usual crowded commuting in the District. After a few days of bitter cold and some light snowfall, the climate had shifted upward on the scale to reach the low sixties. As such, her best protection from the elements was a long-sleeved, button-up shirt with pants. Rain was a fifty-fifty, so her purse included an umbrella. Though for the time, only some medium-gray clouds matted the heavens above. The early afternoon sun still beamed well through the attempted camouflage of the weak overcast.

It was easy for Sheridan to find a space. There were many vacancies. She figured it was because it was Friday. At *The Kensington Post's* headquarters, the number of staff in the office on Fridays was always lighter, with most choosing that as a date for telecommuting. Rumor around the cubicles was that one of the foreign offices did not even bother opening on Fridays, though it was only a rumor. For her part, Roberta preferred going into the office five days a week. She felt more responsible and disciplined when doing so. Though if she felt a need to pick a day to work remotely each week, her selection would be Monday. A good way to ease into the work week, she reasoned.

Purse slung over her shoulder, press badge tucked into her shirt pocket, recorder and digital notepad inside her purse, Roberta got out of the car and headed toward the building where the pregnancy resource center was situated. The name of the center was not on any of the exterior walls; however, her GPS app on her phone showed it to be the correct location. Automatic doors welcomed her in. Sheridan turned off her app when she saw a directory posted by an elevator showing "New Hope Pregnancy Care and Resource Center" listed as occupying the entirety of the third floor.

She pushed a button, and the elevator opened. She was the only one in the box. As no one else was in the hallway, she pressed the button that immediately shut the doors. Roberta selected number three on the board and was at the floor in seconds. Doors opened to a hallway with potted plants and simple carpeting. To her left were two mahogany doors that sort of looked like chocolate bars. Above them was a long rectangular window with the name of the center in all-capital black letters.

Just as Roberta was looking for a way to make her presence known, one of the doors opened. Before her was a silver-haired, older woman—likely in her early to middle sixties—with light blue eyes and a paunchy frame, which was covered by a green dress that went down to her shins. She wore heels, which made her a couple inches taller than the visiting reporter. On one wrist was a piece of jewelry, while the other had a watch that kept track of her heartrate and steps. She exuded acceptance.

"Hello there. Are you Miss Sheridan?" she asked, smiling and approaching the reporter with an outstretched hand.

"Yes, I am."

"Why, hello there. I am Mrs. Lee. A pleasure to meet you," she said, as the two shook hands. "Come on in; come on in."

Roberta obliged, with Lee holding open the door for her to enter the reception room for the center. The reception looked similar to the hallway. There were windows on the right side, which had light semitransparent curtains. The wallpaper featured blue and white stripes, and the room had simple carpeting. There were two plush couches for visitors to sit on, two mantles with stacks of magazines, and two potted ferns that had grown to the average height of an adult male. A grandfather clock was in one corner.

"It will still be another two hours before we open for the day," explained Lee as the two walked by the counter where the receptionist was casually chatting with one of the OB-GYNs who was on staff. "That's why it is a little desolate now." She laughed at her own comment. "Would you like a water or coffee?"

"I'm okay, thank you."

Lee led the reporter as the two turned left into a hallway. It had light brown wallpaper. Between the doors to various rooms hung illustrations of plants, nature, and fruit. Roberta looked to her sides, noticing through open doors examination rooms, a counseling facility with a chair and couch, and an office with four phones for their helpline. Finally, the two turned into one of the offices. "This is my office. I think it will be a good place to talk in private. Is that okay with you?"

"Yes, sure."

Lee's office had a similar theme in its décor to what was seen elsewhere at the center. The carpeting was a light brown; the walls were a calming shade of blue; and the lone window had white curtains so one could partially view the outside world. Her desk had photos of loved ones and a framed prayer from Saint Mother Teresa of Calcutta, with the historic figure's photo image placed beside the text.

"Good, I am glad to hear," replied Lee. "Go ahead and have a seat. Make yourself comfortable. I will be right back." Roberta had her pick of chairs, as there were seats—aside from the one at the desk—that she knew Lee was going to take. One in the corner had metal legs and thin cushions for the back and bottom. Two placed on the opposite side of the desk from where Lee was going to sit were plush, looking to be from the same set as the couches in the waiting room. She chose one of them.

She seemed nice enough, the reporter thought. Roberta unzipped her purse and took out the professional tools. The circular recording device with automatic transcription. The digital notepad with accompanying pen that formatted written letters to guarantee legibility. Both devices were fully powered in advance of the trip out to the center. Just as she turned to the doorway, in came Lee, who closed the door behind her and pushed a button on the knob that created a sign on the other side stating that they were not to be disturbed. It was a common technology for offices that included counseling services.

"Sorry for keeping you waiting," said Lee as she walked across the room to be in front of the seated reporter. "I just had to let the regulars know that I was going to be unavailable for the time being."

"That makes sense."

"So, you are friends with Mr. Chan?"

"Yes, since middle school."

"Aw, that's very nice," she said with sincerity. "Even with social media, I do not usually keep track of my old friends, I am sorry to say."

"Well, I do not keep good track of most of my friends, either, to be fair," assured Roberta, who then changed tone. "Anyway, Mike, that is Mr. Chan, told me that you knew Dr. Hood decades back. Worked alongside him, that is."

"Yes, that is correct."

"Can you give me some background on how that happened?"

"Before I do, can I request that in your article, you identify me with a pseudonym?" asked Lee. "While everyone here knows my past, some of our donors do not. I am sorry to say, but they might not want to provide financial support for the center if they find out that it is headed by a former abortion clinic employee, even one like me who has since renounced abortion."

"Understood. Yes, I can do that."

"Great, thank you," she replied.

"No problem. Is this background going to be on the record?"

"Yes, yes, it can be. Thank you for asking."

Roberta pressed a button and the recorder began its work. "So, Mrs. Lee, how did you first become involved in the abortion industry?"

"Through my father," she responded. "He was, well, I am sorry to say, an abortion performer. Now, now, now, to be clear, he was one of the good ones. You know what I mean? That is, he only did them really early or only for things like when the mother's life was in danger. Bad stuff, I admit, but not as bad as the others. He didn't like it like Dr. Hood did. Anyhoo, my father owned a clinic in California. The West Coast Clinic for Women. It was the one that Dr. Hood eventually took over. In fact, I still have paperwork from the deal. If you like, if it would help your story, I can send you digital copies later today."

"Yes, that would be very helpful."

"Okay, good, I will be happy to help," said Lee, who without prompt returned to the events from her history. "So, I was fresh out of college with a nursing degree. In the past, that was a good degree to have. People were always hiring nurses. There never seemed to be enough of them. However, when I finally completed my degree and my training, it was right in the middle of the whole 'robo-nurse' craze.

Nearly every hospital in the country had switched to automated nursing. Thankfully, my father needed to hire some new nurses for his clinic, and as you can imagine, I got hired pretty quickly."

"I see."

"Now, just to clarify, I did not do any abortions. I couldn't stomach the idea, even back when I supported the practice." She laughed at the absurdity that she once held such a position on abortion, then continued. "So, anyhow, I worked there. Mostly, I helped the patients before and after the procedure. You know, comfort, health check. Like I said, my father was one of the better ones. He at least made sure they got a good checkup before we let them go. That kind of stuff."

"And when did Dr. Hood show up?"

"He came on staff about a year after I did. A dashing young man. Brown hair. Brown eyes. Plump nose. He always joked about it; I think he didn't like it. I thought it was kind of cute, to be honest. It fit, if nothing else. Honestly—and I do not know if I want this on the record—but for a time, you know, I kind of had a thing for him. We were both single back then, so there was nothing sinful about it. But, um, yeah . . . maybe that shouldn't be on the record. What do you think, Miss Sheridan?"

"Since I will be using a pseudonym . . . "

"You know what, in that case, sure, keep it," she said, laughing a little before she returned to the past. "Point is, we, um . . . that is, we worked alongside each other quite a bit. And for a couple years, at least two. We knew each other. He used to tell me about his experiences, chopping them up and researching the pieces. When I told him to stop, he was surprised but respected my wishes. I guess you could say he was nice. To me and others at least. Maybe because we were already born." She giggled at her own remark. Sheridan gave a faint smile to commend the effort.

"When did you two part ways?"

"That started on the day Roe v. Wade was overturned. It was really something. We barely got any work done that day. Few women came in. I think it was because since so many folks just knew it was going to happen, no one wanted to be caught in an abortion clinic. Just in case abortion got outlawed immediately. But we were all anxiously awaiting the release of the result. It came out later than most decisions. Usually, because of the time difference, we folk in California wake up to the news. But not that one; it seemed to take forever for it to be released. Half the staff checked the blogs, while the rest of us were in the waiting room watching the TV." Lee paused. "You know what a TV is, right?"

"Yes, my grandparents have one."

"Oh, okay, good, had to make sure," she said. "Anyways, we were all nervous. Because we just knew the decision was going to be against us. How could it not be? Still, there was a nerve of hope that kept us from total despair. A little bit of optimism that the Supreme Court was going to reaffirm the precedent. We were wrong, of course." She laughed some more. "Today, I can't even believe it—that I was so terrified at the idea of abortion being banned. A different world. Anyway . . . I don't remember who found out first. It seemed like the blogs and the news channel reported it at the same time. The decision, that is. We were all stunned. Not because we didn't see it coming, but because it was the worst-case scenario. Our biggest fear was reality. Permanent. Immutable."

"How did Dr. Hood react?"

"Quietly," recalled Lee. "He went back to his office, closed the door, and that was that for about an hour. No one wanted to bother him. We all felt awful. After an hour or so, he came out and informed us that we were closing. He heard rumors among other abortion providers that violent protesters were coming our way. He was afraid for our well-being. He didn't want us to be victims. So, we all agreed to leave the place. It turned out to be false. No riots happened around us. To the contrary, a ton of activists formed a human wall of protection around us, pretty much all day and night. As a result, we were open up until the National Guard showed up and forced us to close down."

"And that was the last time you saw Dr. Hood."

"Correct," she nodded. "And I thought it would be the last time I ever saw him. Not just because he disappeared but because I moved on. With the clinic closed, I needed work. Thankfully, a hospital out in Northern Virginia had decided to phase out their robo-nurses. As you may be aware, many studies released around that time found little difference in the recovery rate for people in hospitals fully staffed by robo-nurses. They found that human nurses provided certain intangible benefits to patients that robotic devices were incapable of giving. With my background and training, they hired me immediately. So I moved out here; eventually found Tyson, my husband; got married; and soon after, we had our first boy. For two years, I knew I would never see Dr. Hood again."

"Then what happened?"

"It was one evening. You see, until I started here, I used to work three 12-hour shifts a week at that hospital. One night, I was coming in late, but I didn't want to go to bed just yet. So I got a drink from the refrigerator, turned on the TV, and just watched whatever. I honestly do not remember what I was watching; I just remember that commercial. It was a campaign ad featuring a Dr. Benjamin Pettus, who was running for Fairfax County Board of Supervisors. That was where things started to feel weird. There was something about him that seemed familiar. Obviously, he looked nothing like Dr. Hood. But he sure sounded like him. At first, I just dismissed it as drowsiness. But then, later that week, I saw another Pettus campaign ad. And another. Even then, though, while it felt weird, I still thought that maybe it was just that he was from the same place. Honestly, I kept thinking, Wow, this Pettus guy sounds just like Dr. Hood. I wonder if they're from the same home town." Remembering her first impression made her laugh for a few moments.

"So, you found out that Pettus was Hood through a campaign ad?"

Lee shook her head. "Oh no, that was just the beginning. As the weeks passed, the ads did get me suspicious. But I was skeptical. After all, Pettus looks nothing like Hood. He doesn't even have that adorably plump nose." Sheridan smirked at the remark. "Then came the moment after the election when I knew it was him. He was holding a press conference at my hospital. It was about a new wing that had just been completed. Pettus—that is, Hood—had been a big advocate for the expansion. I remember liking him for that. Anyway, he showed up and we nurses and doctors all got to meet him." Lee suddenly became very concentrated, sincere, driven, her words more pounding. "When I finally got to meet him, shake his hand, that was when I knew it was him. And I knew it because of how he reacted. The hesitation, the nervousness, the slight discomfort. And that look. The look he gave me, like he knew it was me. Like we had met before. Like he was afraid I would figure it out and tell everyone there, shouting it as loud as I could. That kind of fear." She returned to her previous tone. "If you can, find the video of the press conference. He was clearly off his game. Stuttering, hesitant, losing his place as he gave his speech. I'm surprised I kept silent."

"Did you tell anyone at the time?"

"My husband. And my priest. That was it, though. I just knew I was never going to vote for him again. I was also never going to vote for his party again. Never really liked the liberal agenda, but I definitely liked it less after he became connected to it."

It sounded believable, but Roberta was still critical. She kept her doubts hidden inside her mind, hinting at them as she asked her next question. "Senator Pettus was elected to the Supervisors Board about thirty-five years ago. Why did you keep silent until now?"

"The amnesty," Lee responded. "The one they gave to abortion providers not long after Roe was overturned. If you read the text, it does not literally give personnel like nurses and secretaries the same clean slate as it does the doctors. It was, I'm sorry to say, at best, implied. It was not until last year that Congress finally voted to clarify the amnesty to include people like me. So now, I don't have to worry about being arrested."

"I see."

"I know he can't go to prison for his crimes, but the least I can do is ruin his public career. For the sake of justice and for the sake of getting that awful healthcare law that he co-sponsored repealed."

Roberta turned off the recorder when the silence indicated that Lee was done with her comments. "Thank you for taking the time to speak with me."

"So, when will the article be published, if you don't mind me asking?"

"I do not know for sure. I will have to do my share of additional research. And whatever else you can send me for my story would be much appreciated."

"Sure thing," said Lee as she opened the door, which automatically turned off the door sign. The two turned left into the hallway, going toward the exit. "I am very thankful that you came here to speak with me. I feel very strongly about this. I cannot wait to read your story."

. . . . . .

"Is this an old pizza?" asked Roberta Sheridan, her words slowed by disgust. She was at Michael Chan's apartment, standing between the couch and a flat screen. She was holding a trash bag with one hand, having already thrown several disposable items into the rubbery black abyss. She had just confirmed the relative cleanliness of that section of the living room before turning to face the couch and nearly stepping on the box. With her free hand, she flipped open the box to reveal three slices topped with pepperoni.

"It's not that old," responded Michael, defensively. He was standing in the archway between the living room and the dining room. The latter space had a small card table in the middle, with four seats tucked under the top.

"How old?"

"Maybe a day or two."

"Definitely trash," she ruled, closing the box and then dropping the mix of bread and cardboard into the black bag before Michael was able to offer protest. "I will never understand why you men do stuff like that."

"Convenience."

"Convenience?" she asked in disbelief.

"Whenever I want a snack and don't feel like going to the kitchen, there it is. Convenience."

"Disgusting," stated Roberta, walking around the couch to see about other waste. Michael shrugged and kept sweeping in the dining room. His sweeper, common for domestic hygiene, was able to thoroughly purge a floor of dirt, dust, and other items while also sucking up small objects like crumbs—all while being silent.

"Thanks again for stopping by to help me with tidying up the place. I mean, I doubt that Helen and I will be coming back to my place; but if we did, I would like to put up a good show, you know?"

"No problem," she said after picking up a food wrapper. "And I agree, it is very unlikely she'll be coming here. Yet still, this place needed a good cleanup."

"That was also my thought," said Michael, who was lowering the angle of the sweep to get at the floor below the card table. "And you always seem to see things I miss."

She sniffed the air. She repeated her action. Then, going where she thought the bizarre aroma emanated from, she looked behind an old frontier chest that once traversed the nation in a covered wagon. "What . . . on earth . . . is that?"

Michael quickly turned the sweeper off, and then he leaned it against the wall. He walked into the living room to stand beside a straightened Roberta, her head slightly angled down and a finger pointing at the object. Again, Michael seemed unmoved by the drama. "Well, I was wondering where that smell was coming from." Roberta was not quite sure what kind of rodent or large bug it used to be. She just knew it was dead. Without a fuss, Michael took the trash bag from Roberta, covered his palm and fingers with some paper towels, and placed the wretched thing into the bag. "I guess this bag is ready to go out to the dumpster. Good eye and good nose, Berta."

"How . . . how did you not smell that?"

"Aroma system," explained Michael, stating the obvious. "Never live alone without one."

"I suggest you turn it off every so often, just in case."

"I will take that under advisement."

"And keep your pizza inside a refrigerator."

"I will also take that under advisement."

"Okay," began Roberta as Michael closed the bag, secured it, and then placed it next to two others at the kitchen entrance door, never leaving the auditory range of his friend. "All right, so, we cleaned up the kitchen, the dining room, the bathroom with the exception of the tub . . . "

"And I will do the toilet a little later."

"Yes," she agreed, pointing at him briefly for the remark. "And now you just need to sweep this room—and, of course, do the toilet, and keep your bedroom door shut—and that should be it. Are we missing anything?"

"No, that was everything."

"Okay, good." She looked at the couch. "I am sitting down now."

"Go ahead. It'll make it easier for me to sweep this room."

She smiled at the remark as she sat down on the couch and then stretched out upon it. "This wasn't as hard as I thought it would be."

"I try," replied Michael, fetching the sweeper from the dining room and then getting to work in the living room, making the floors look as clean as they did the day he moved in. "Thanks again for helping."

"No problem. You gave me something to do after my jog to keep myself active. You know after running several miles, you're supposed to walk around some more to hinder soreness."

"Interesting. I didn't know that."

"Well, keep it in mind if you ever take my offer to jog with that group I meet with every Saturday morning."

"Yeah, sure," said Michael as he had a third of the room swept. His apprehension was elevated as he continued. "So, Berta, I heard you got to talk with Etna yesterday."

"I did."

Michael expected more of a response. His friend was leaning back on the throw pillows on the couch. She had put a few alongside one of the arms to cushion her relaxing lean. "So, um, what did you think? Do we have a story?"

"Maybe."

"Wait, maybe?" asked Michael, stopping halfway through his sweeping. "What do you mean by 'maybe'?"

"Well, I haven't made up my mind."

"What is the problem?"

"Well, she has a lot going for her," began Roberta. "She seems honest; her account has details; and she had a plausible explanation for why it took her so long to reach out."

Roberta stopped speaking. Michael felt awkward. "Well, then, what was the problem?"

"Problems," she corrected. "There were multiple issues. First one being that she was pushing a memory of thirty-five to forty years, give or take. Second, her evidence is that she thinks Senator Pettus sounds like Dr. Hood and appeared to be nervous when he first met her in Virginia. This is all conjecture, innuendo, etcetera. Third, she has no corroboration for her anecdotes. No one is there to confirm her story or her claims. Fourth, she is biased politically. She's conservative, Pettus is liberal."

"That doesn't mean she is wrong."

"True, but it makes for a hard sell. Both for me and my editor. To say nothing of Pettus supporters should they read my story."

"Clara Grant."

"The activist? What about her?"

"She knew Etna. Knows her, in fact," countered Michael, both hands resting on the top of the sweeper. "Like a good citizen journalist, I asked Lee about evidence, eye-witnesses, all that. She told me that Ms. Grant had an abortion at her clinic. That she can bear witness to a lot of what Etna said to both of us."

"That can help."

"Good."

"Hopefully, my editor will agree. So far, she is as much on the fence about this allegation as I am. And to be honest, I am not sure Grant is the best character witness. After all, she may hold many of the same viewpoints as Pettus, but she is still a divisive firebrand that automatically turns off a lot of folks."

"That doesn't mean she is wrong."

"Yes, you are right. And I am still planning to interview her. After all, if her story checks out, that makes the accusation bipartisan. Yet still, there needs to be more work. We cannot expect something well-grounded based off of the claims of an old right-winger and an inflammatory community activist."

"You have a lot of doubts," conceded Michael. "But I think we can remove them with time and research."

"Right now, there are only a few unresolved things that keep me from quitting this assignment."

"You mean, stuff like Pettus' lost history, the age and voice similarities? That stuff?"

"Yes, plus one more."

"What would that be?"

"Lee talked about there being a vote last year to broaden the wording of the amnesty to specifically include nurses and secretaries."

"Yeah. What about it?"

"I looked up the legislation's history . . . Pettus voted against it."

CHAPTER 4

CLARA GRANT HAD SPOKEN BEFORE several county governments and school boards. It was a hobby at first. She had a regular full time job, in addition to raising children. However, she had reached retirement age a few years ago, and the children were all grown. And so, her social justice activism became a greater focus for her life. She traveled across the United States, able to speak at divers places in short amounts of time due to advances in faster trains and speedier planes. She lived in an age where it took two hours to fly from coast to coast and well below that from coast to Midwest.

Among them all, Grant rarely encountered a meeting place as Spartan as the board of education meeting she was set to attend. No elegant backdrop behind the board members, no intricate carvings, nor historic pieces. This meeting was held on a theater stage. Large, dark blue curtains were closed behind them, with three thin, wooden folding tables placed end to end for the members to sit at. A lone banner draped over the center table gave the name of the school district, as well as its logo of a prowling tiger. Two flags were positioned next to the opposite sides of the tables, kept up with two bronze stands.

Grant saw the board members taking their seats, with intermittent casual talk breaking out as the time for the meeting to commence was drawing nigh. Aside from the board members, there was a secretary present to take minutes. The role was largely symbolic. All the figure did was place a small rectangular recording device on the end of the table and push a button. The device perfectly recorded the meeting, transcribed it with near-perfect accuracy, and automatically submitted the notes to the archives the moment the recording was turned off. A single camera, which was programmed to automatically direct itself to face whomever was speaking, likewise was largely independent of human need. The cameraman need only verify that the device was capturing the correct speaker and to turn it on and off as needed. Once the meeting was concluded, upon being turned off, it likewise sent a copy of the visual recording to the archives and also automatically sent a copy to the school district's website for viewing online. This did not include the livestream on social media and on local streaming channels.

Grant rose from her seat like the others around her and those on the stage. Everyone turned themselves to behold the flag of the United States of America. Nearly everyone, including all on the stage, placed their hands over their hearts and recited the Pledge. Grant was among them. From there, the board recognized a moment of silence for meditation, prayer, contemplation, or, in the case of Grant, to center herself on the task to come. Moment concluded, all were told to be seated.

The board president went over the old business. These were minor matters—talk of progress on constructing a new gym for a middle school, an update on the financial status of a free lunch program for the less fortunate. From there, the board agreed to go into new business. Grant's proposal was not the first on the agenda. Rather, a resolution to recognize Women's History Month was brought before the board. The resolution had nineteen whereas clauses, to represent the Nineteenth Amendment. The new business was quickly approved, with the board voice voting the measure.

"And our next order of business will be a proposed resolution brought to us by a Mrs. Clara Grant," said the board president. Like most of the audience for the meeting, the president was a Muslim-American with Middle Eastern ancestry but was born and had lived nearly all of her life in the United States.

Grant rose from her seat, located in the row before the front line. It was a habit she had maintained when going to church and figuring which pew to sit in. She shuffled by two folks sitting to her right, expressing the usual pardons for having to squeeze by them. From there, she walked a brief distance to a podium placed between the front row of bolted theater seats and the stage. Attached to the podium was a small circular device, three inches in diameter. She pushed the device, signaling the camera to focus on her and also making her voice louder as though amplified by a microphone.

"Good evening, members of the board, president and vice president of the board. I come to you this evening hoping to right a historical wrong. We know that whenever an oppressive institution is vanquished, it keeps vestiges around. These symbols of a dark, horrid past need to be erased. By having them on our maps or our buildings or as statues in our parks, we give voice to deplorable, unacceptable practices. Our society should not be condoning the worst of our former ways.

"To wit, I submit for your consideration a petition signed by over twenty-thousand students and parents and teachers calling for the changing of the name of Barack Obama Elementary School. We understand why the school received the name that it did. Obama made history long ago when he became the first African-American president of the United States. However, making history does not negate the truly awful things he stood for. It is a matter of public record that Obama instituted pro-abortion policies while in office. He actively funded the murdering of babies, the most vulnerable of our society. And as president, he constantly undermined efforts to restrict or abolish the barbarous practice.

"Now some would say that his milestone in racial civil rights compensates for his failures regarding the rights of the unborn. I say that is not good enough. Roger Taney made history when he became the first Roman Catholic Supreme Court Justice. He made history again when he became the first Roman Catholic Chief Justice. And yet, these milestones in religious civil rights and religious pluralism do not compensate for his morally bankrupt ruling in *Dred Scott v. Sandford.*"

Grant had put down her remarks in a file on her mobile phone. She rarely looked down, as she had the speech basically memorized. Though she looked down more as she got to the details of the Antebellum case. "In that despicable ruling, Taney wrote the majority opinion, refusing to recognize the inherent worth of African-Americans. As he said—and I give apologies for the archaic language—'a free negro of the African race, whose ancestors were brought to this country and sold as slaves, is not a citizen within the meaning of the Constitution of the United States.' This evil was recognized for what it is by more modern minds. As a result, Taney has been justly punished by having his name removed from many of the places that once honored him for his religious minority milestone.

"For most of us, it is an easy task to switch out African-Americans for the unborn and the denial of citizenship for the denial of the right to life. And so it should be obvious that we can switch Taney for Obama and make the same well-informed decision. Students are free to learn about Obama, and there will be times when he should be acknowledged for his historic success. However, his success led to the deaths of millions through his domestic policies. And in his cruel devotion to that genocidal act, as any presidential historian can tell you, he sought to curb the religious rights of many minority groups so that others opposed to abortion were being forced to fund the deplorable procedure.

"Members of the board, Mrs. President and Mr. Vice President, I implore you to stand on the right side of history and remove the last vestiges of a savage age from our school system. I have two lovely grandchildren who attend Obama Elementary. When they learned about the evil of the Obama administration, they asked their mother, my daughter, 'How can we celebrate a baby-killer and consider ourselves the good guys?' Well, I say, you are all good guys. And you all know what is the best thing to do here."

. . . . . .

Roberta Sheridan was getting ready for an interview. She was located in her cubicle. Originally, she and the interviewee were going to meet in person. The figure was in the District of Columbia for a rally in support of the healthcare law, so the distance was minimal. However, something came up, leading to a need to reschedule and then a need to do the conversation remotely. Roberta agreed to the decision. Most of her interviews were done from the cubicle anyway. This was not a special occurrence.

Roberta had her questions printed on a digital pad beside her computer. Though she already had the query pretty well captured in her mind, she wanted something nearby just in case. It reminded her of her early years in church, before she belonged to a congregation that used projection screens. While she had classics by Michael W. Smith and Chris Tomlin fairly well memorized, she liked to have the hymnal open to the correct page as insurance. The computer screen featured the phone device to call the person of interest. Her recorder was wirelessly connected to the keyboard, thus allowing the conversation to be recorded and transcribed without fear of office interference.

According to her office clock, the time for the scheduled interview had arrived. However, Roberta was intentionally planning to be a minute or two late. She learned through past experience that calling exactly on the scheduled moment did not work. After all, sometimes the interviewee had a slower clock or was not yet ready despite the mutually agreed upon time slot. "Trust in the Lord; He will deliver you," she quietly spoke. "Have faith in the Lord; He will see you through." Then she pushed the buttons on the temporal screen to select visual conversation, as opposed to audio only, and called the interviewee.

After a few rings, the face of Clara Grant appeared on her screen. She was at her place in New Jersey, having arrived there only an hour before. It had taken less time than that for the rail system to bring her from D.C. to her home. She had the look of a kindly grandmother, albeit with a hint of fire in her eyes. There were some brief distortions in the image, but otherwise the quality of the projection made her look like she was there in person. Roberta began the conversation.

"Good morning, Mrs. Grant."

"Good morning."

"As you know, we are scheduled for an interview at this time."

"Yes, correct," she said. "And let me just say that I am sorry I had to cancel on you at first. Even with the speed of the rails, I found myself with too much stuff going on at once."

"That's okay, understood," encouraged Roberta. "I am glad that you can talk to me now about my story."

"Yes, definitely."

"So, just to start off my questions," began Roberta, Grant nodding in approval. "As I understand, you know Etna Lee, right?"

"That's correct."

"Can you tell me, for background purposes, how you two first met?"

"Yes, I can," she said, becoming more somber. "I confess that it is not a better time in my life, but we first met back in California. You see, as you may or may not know, I once had an abortion." She paused before continuing. "That was when they were still legal and when I still thought they were acceptable. It was none other than Dr. Hood who performed it while Lee looked after me before and after the procedure."

"I see," noted Roberta. "Would you mind explaining the specific events, if you are comfortable with giving such details?"

"Sure, sure, I can do that," Grant immediately replied, nearly cutting off the reporter. "After all, I have talked about my abortion in the past. It was, as I said, decades ago. A different time. I was working at a cosmetic surgery center out in Los Angeles. After a one-night-stand one weekend, I found myself pregnant and with no man around to help with bills. At first, I thought I could handle the possible expenses.

But then I realized that I could barely support myself, let alone another person.

"If I had to make the decision today, I would have just put the child up for adoption. They always forgot to talk about that—adoption. It was as though my only two options were poverty or abortion. That was the dichotomy they gave me. So, on the advice of a friend who had had an abortion the year before, I went to Hood's West Coast Clinic. I was in my second trimester at the time, and I heard he was very good at later-term abortions. So, I drove down and entered the clinic. After I filled out a form and went to this one office, Etna came in and prepped me for things. She was very nice, told me she understood that I must be nervous but that everything would be okay. That sort of stuff.

"Then came the procedure. I was conscious the whole time, but not in pain. They gave me something to dull everything. Still, I could feel the objects being used on me. The injection that turned my womb into a gas chamber. The tongs as they were guided into me and pulled stuff out. The vacuum as it thudded into me to remove the rest. The part that always sticks with me, the part I cannot un-see, was near the end of the procedure. I turned my head to look at a table to the side." She took a breath before continuing. For a time, it seemed like she was going to lose her composure, but Grant maintained her stability. "On the table . . . on the table, there was a metal pan. It looked like something one uses to bake stuff in an old oven. On it were the pieces. Little limbs, a part of a head. I never forgot that. I never will. That was the first time I truly started to hate abortionism."

"I am sorry about your experiences," said Roberta. "And I appreciate you telling me about them for my story."

"Sure, no problem," Grant replied. "As I said, Lee visited me after the procedure. She made sure that I was in good health before I left the clinic. We kept in touch a little in the years following. She was happy that I was getting better. We did fall out of touch for about a few years after she moved away."

"When did you reconnect?"

"Twelve years ago. I was attending a Remembrance Day event at the Basilica of the National Shrine of the Immaculate Conception. That year, the theme was women who regretted their abortions. I very clearly fit the bill. After the observance, I tripped on a sidewalk and landed badly. Bad enough that I had to go to the hospital. And it just so happened that the very first nurse to check on me was Etna Lee. It only took us a few moments to recall where we had seen each other before. So yes, to answer your question, Etna definitely worked at Hood's clinic. I remember her then; I remember her now."

"So when she says that Senator Benjamin Pettus is Edgar Hood, do you believe her?"

"Yes, without question, I believe her," Grant said, absent any hesitation. "I trust Etna very much. I have never known her to lie. And I might add, there was an incident I started to remember when you first reached out to me. It was a strange bit of correspondence I got from Hood not long before he disappeared."

"What did he say?"

"Well, it was strange," began Grant. "He emailed me around the time the president announced that the military was going to force California to follow the anti-Roe decision. I first wondered how he even got my email address, though soon enough I realized that, well, of course he would have it, since Etna worked for him. He explained—in his email, that is—that he was looking to get cosmetic work done and asked if my company could do it. At first, I thought he just wanted to fix his nose. In my opinion, it was his one blemish. But in a follow-up email, he talked about wanting to do a lot of stuff."

"What kind of stuff?"

"His nose, his hair, and most odd of all, his eyes," replied Grant, causing Roberta to become more conspiratorial in her contemplations. "He asked for permanent alterations to his eyes. I told him that unfortunately, my employer was not qualified for such a complex surgery, but I did give him references. Then he asked me something weirder."

"Weirder?"

"Yes, something that made total sense later on," noted Grant. "He wanted to know if any of my references also did fingerprint work."

"Fingerprint work? As in, changing his fingerprints?"

"Yes, exactly. Back then, it was still legal in some states."

"I see."

"As if that was not weird enough, he then asked something really weird."

"Really weird?"

"Yes, more strange. He was—and I still cannot believe he was—but he actually asked me if any of my coworkers had been infected by the Ultralord Virus. I knew of one. From there, he actually asked me if that coworker could forward him the email that triggered the virus on her files. I was totally shocked. I was like 'Why in the world would you want that?' Of course, again, when I learned that he disappeared, I knew the answer."

"Do you still have the correspondence between yourself and Dr. Hood?"

"Yes, I do," replied Grant. "I can forward it to you later today if you like."

"Yes, definitely," responded Sheridan. "Also, if you have the list of references from back then, you know, of other cosmetic surgeons . . ."

"Yes, yes," agreed Grant. "Actually, those will be included in the forwarded correspondence."

"Okay, very good, thank you. And thank you for getting back to me about my questions."

"You are welcome," said Grant. "If you need anything else, do not hesitate to call me."

. . . . . .

"Are you sure that you are not interested in my extra ticket?" asked Andrew McClellan, as he socialized with Roberta in his cubicle. Both stood on opposite ends of the opening, with McClellan keeping an eye on his computer screen.

"What would your wife say?"

"Ha-ha," he deadpanned. "You know that eight other folks are coming, including my wife."

"Still, I'm not really interested," she begged off. "To be honest, I have never really been a big fan of Charolash. The whole Zoom Rock craze just seems a little too trendy, you know?"

"You know, Suarez told me you liked Dee-O Dee-O better."

"That's because they are a better band."

"Is that a fact?" asked McClellan, playfully pensive.

"Better sales, better reviews," countered Roberta. "Those are facts."

"Regardless, you know stuff like this is just as much about the socializing as it is the music."

"Provided they give you noise-cancelers."

"Even without them, we're all planning to meet up beforehand and have dinner," said McClellan, raising his finger to make the second point. "And not to play matchmaker, but a buddy of mine who still works at *The Courier* will be there. I think you two might be, you know, compatible."

"Oh, Drew," Roberta began. "That would be a serious ethical violation."

"Why?"

"Dating the enemy?"

"Oh, come on," he said, brushing the air with his hand. "You know only the editors take that whole rivalry seriously. And they make nice when it matters."

"All right, I'll think about it," she said. "And I might even wear my Dee-O Dee-O shirt for the fun of it."

McClellan smiled. Then out of the corner of his eye, he noticed an alert coming on his screen. Roberta continued to lean on her end of the cubicle wall while he went back to his seat to check the notification. "It is our luddite boss. She wants me to tell you to get to her office."

"All right, tell her I am on my way."

Roberta first went to her cubicle. The topic for the meeting was already known. Jocelyn Lopez explained in the morning chat that she was going to check in on the progress of the various feature stories that each journalist under her watch was working on. Roberta got to her workspace, taking her digital notepad with its notes on the matter, as well as a pen that was able to write on the device. All supplies ready, she walked the several feet from her space to the open portal of her editor's office. She knocked lightly on the door, the noise drawing Lopez's attention. The editor looked away from the two keyboard projections and beckoned Roberta into the room.

"Come on in and sit down," she said without malice. Her eyes went back to the screen on her right, as she put the last touches on a submission. The alterations finalized, she clicked a button that published the article on *The Kensington Post's* website. Once this was accomplished, she exited out of both screens, prompting both to disappear. This allowed her to bestow full attention to her subordinate. "Before we begin, I feel a need to remind you that it is 'Women's History Month,' not 'Woman's History Month.'"

Roberta was embarrassed. "Did I make that mistake again?"

"Yes. Twice in your last article."

"Sorry," she replied. "I'll post a note on my cubicle wall."

"Whatever works," Lopez said with encouragement. "Now, tell me about how your research is working on your investigative piece."

"Well, I am making progress," began Roberta. "I just finished up my second interview, this time with Clara Grant."

"The Clara Grant, I assume?"

"Yes."

"What did she have to say?"

"She confirmed that Etna Lee did, in fact, work at the West Coast Clinic for Women. She also told me about how Hood contacted her at one point to see about getting plastic surgery and purposely getting infected by the Ultralord Virus."

"Okay, that sounds interesting," the editor noted, speaking as though she were a therapist. "And did Grant have any evidence of her own besides memories?"

"Yes, a goodly amount at that," replied the journalist. "She forwarded me email correspondence between her and Hood all about this talk of plastic surgery. And she even sent me a list of places she told Hood about. Earlier today, I sent out some queries to the ones that are still open. Maybe they can give me more information."

"That makes sense," Lopez nodded. "And what are your next steps for the story?"

"Well, I am going to try and find the plastic surgery place that might have worked on Hood. See what they can tell me. Hopefully. I also plan to reach out to Linda Harrison for background research, and possibly another lede."

"Linda Harrison?"

"The hacker who created Ultralord."

"Oh, right, right. For some reason, I keep forgetting that the hacker was a woman. My 'woke' grandmother would be ashamed of me."

"For what it's worth, it surprised me, too."

"Well," Lopez began, "It sounds like you have made a lot of progress. I am glad that you now have two sources who have provided details. And they are polar political opposites. I am also glad that you are continuing to dig. I advise that, when the time is appropriate, you broaden the search to other surgical businesses. It is very possible that if Hood did what you and Chan think he did, he might not have used one of the referrals."

"Very true."

"All in all, I like your progress."

"Good, I'm glad."

"I just have one problem, unfortunately," cautioned Lopez, prompting Roberta to have a great change in mood.

. . . . . .

Roberta left her apartment per the usual time on that Saturday morning. The weather was about twice as warm as it had been the Saturday before. As a result, she wore shorts and a t-shirt rather than her running tights and a long-sleeved shirt. On her left wrist, she had on a device that tracked her speed and distance. Resembling a wrist watch, the device also uploaded the varying route for each Saturday into its system, giving vocal directions as Roberta ran through the neighborhood with the others. A sports drink patch attached to her upper left arm for once she started perspiring would gradually feed her body the necessary chemicals to stay hydrated and healthy. The patch was a commonly used hydration device for athletes, amateur and professional. She also had a small bag with a zipped pocket that contained her keys, photo ID, and a twenty-dollar bill in the event she ate out afterwards.

It was a social media group that met offline to run in the District of Columbia. About three hundred followed the group; however, attendance was usually between twenty and forty. Roberta was a regular. Since joining the runners' group two years ago, she only missed five meetups. Three of them were because of family gatherings, while the other two clashed with work assignments. She and the chief organizers were on a first name basis, and she sometimes forwent running to help with the support and gear stations, or SAGs for short.

While the routes varied each week, they always met at the same park. The location was about six blocks from where Roberta lived. She was the only one who walked to the park. Everyone else lived too far away. The majority of the group members lived in Northern Virginia or Southern Maryland. To many, the selection of the D.C. park for the weekly jog served as a nice compromise. During the darker, colder half of the year, they arrived at 8:00 a.m. During the hotter, brighter half, 7:00 a.m.

Roberta neared the corner eleven minutes before eight, cars coming up from her left side to slow down and turn into a convenient adjacent lot. Entering the park, she found her peers. Most were within five to ten years of her age. One regular was actually in his fifties, yet fared well when running with those born after his generation. There were a few married couples and a few unmarried couples. Among the regulars were a mother-daughter duo, the former in her forties, while the latter was college-aged. Roberta mingled as the time for the start of the jog drew ever closer.

"How are you, Barb?" she asked one of the women.

"Doing fine, Roberta. I absolutely love this weather."

"Well, just remember, it might not be as nice two miles in."

"There is that," Barbara conceded.

Joey, one of the organizers, was a forty-something with a brown beard that had touches of gray. He was skinny, yet muscular, having four marathons and seven half-marathons on his list of accomplishments. With a booming voice, he called together the various folks in fitness wear, with timers and digital copies of course directions. There were thirty-two people that morning, no doubt inspired by the pleasant climate to show up. A few softer conversations continued as he gave out the key points.

"First of all, there will be two routes this morning: a five-miler and a ten-miler. Now how many of you all are the doing the five?" Twenty hands went up, Roberta's among them. "And how many of you are doing ten?" Eleven hands, including Joey's, came up. "And how many of you are doing something in between?" The remaining jogger raised his hand, as he had explained earlier that he was doing eight miles. "Okay then. There is a SAG stationed at the intersection of Sherman and Rhode Island. You ten-milers are going to go by it twice. So, make sure you tell Abby and Baker your route as you go by, so they know to see you again." There were nods and thumbs ups in response. "Okay, then. Let's get going!"

"Are you going to speed through this one or take it easy?" Barbara asked Roberta as the two were walking toward the street with the group.

"I think I will try to keep it below nine minutes a mile. You?"

"I'll try to keep pace with you," she said. "At least until we get to the SAG."

"Of course," said Roberta, smiling.

Like a herd, they turned as a group onto the street, pressing devices to start their count on time and distance. Many were starting at a leisurely pace, keeping to the advice of making the first one or two miles their slowest. Both routes, as well as the individual doing eight, started out with the same first few streets. Then the folks started to part ways, with that minority of longer distance runners peeling off to the right while the majority, including Roberta and Barbara, continued straight.

Less than forty-five minutes later, the two friends returned to the park. Their respective devices beeped in near unison at the completion of their exercise. Both confirmed the signal by each pushing buttons that stopped the tracking. Barbara was more winded than Roberta. This was likely due to her deciding to catch up to Roberta after stopping at the SAG for a minute. Either way, Roberta patted her on the back for encouragement. Others were trickling in as well, including Joey, who was the first ten-miler to make it back. He set about positively supporting the others, offering applause and assurance that they were doing great. After a little bit of socializing, Roberta said her goodbyes and began to walk back to her apartment, graciously declining a ride by Barbara.

A warm morning felt all the hotter as Roberta wiped away the sweat from her forehead. Even with the scanter exercise attire, she glistened, darkening corners of her clothes with the perspiration. She felt strength from the accomplishment as her body finished off the last of the red sports liquid in the patch. An advanced model, it had its own cooling system, allowing the fluid to feel even better when it entered her body. Refreshing, empowering, emboldened. Always a good way to start her weekend.

Unlike earlier when she was running in the streets, she did not need to pay attention to the passing vehicles as she occupied the sidewalk instead. However, the next vehicle to come from behind slowed down, the driver lightly honking his horn. Curious, she turned to see the automobile and beheld a familiar person behind the wheel. She stopped, a hand to each hip and gave a smirk. Michael Chan smiled and waved, his black compact stopped in the middle of the road, though with no one behind him.

"You want a ride?"

"No thanks, Mike," she shouted back.

"I insist. Come on."

"Oh, okay," Roberta conceded, walking across the front of the vehicle to get to the passenger door. The jogger got inside just as another car turned onto the road. Michael accelerated away before the other vehicle could get close.

"I was on my way to the diner, and I wanted to take you with me."

"Really? Won't your girlfriend get jealous?"

"Helen works at the diner," he replied. "That's how we met."

"Ah."

"Besides, I think I need a second opinion on her. You know, a good critical eye," he explained as he was compelled to stop due to a red light.

"Fair enough, but I would like to shower and change before I show up."

"If you like," agreed Michael. "So, how's the story coming?"

"The Hood one, right?"

"Yeah, what else? Did you get to talk to Grant?"

"I did get to talk to her earlier this week. And she gave me some good info. Plenty of stuff to work with. There is definitely progress, and Jocelyn thinks things are going well."

"I am sensing a 'but' coming up," Michael stated as the light went green and he went forward.

"You know, it is primary season, Mike. You know my beat is politics. Jocelyn told me that I have to put my story on hold for a month or two."

"You've got to be kidding me."

"No joke, Mike."

"I don't understand," began a visibly upset Michael. "Berta, you said we were doing well; you said she liked it. And now she says stop it?"

"Delay, not stop," clarified Roberta as her apartment complex came into view. "She still wants me to look into it, but it has to wait."

"For two months?"

"It's just as well. Part of my story is to interview Linda Harrison, and she won't be available for an in-person interview for several weeks. Something about planning it ahead, making sure certain security measures are taken."

"I see."

"Mike, listen . . . " she began to say, but then halted as Michael stopped the car in front of her apartment building. "We can talk about it more over breakfast. Okay?"

"Okay," he agreed. His mood started to lighten. "How quick can you get ready?"

"Ten, maybe fifteen minutes."

"Okay, I'll go around the block a few times."

"Thanks, Mike," she replied as she exited the car and slammed the door. An optimistic wave with a smile was given to Michael as she rushed to the front of the building, took out her key, opened the entrance, and hurried in to get ready with expedience.

CHAPTER 5

IT WAS LIKE SO MANY political rallies of its time. The format was the same—a large conference room with an impressive platform constructed on one side. It had a pattern of flags at the back, every other one being the state flag and then the national flag. Numerous clusters of balloons—red, white, and blue—placed all over. Holographic fireworks splashed on the ceiling, and amid the open floor in front of the elevated platform were the technological streamers far easier to clean than their paper ancestors.

Contemporary patriotic music shared the audio canopy with classic hits from the mid-to- late twentieth century and some from the early twenty-first. Attendees ranged in age and fashion, though most were older and in proper attire. Though, to be sure, many were youths, and some wore jeans. There were several cameras perched at various points. Anymore, the talking head in front of the lens had the knowledge to set up the camera, and the device effectively governed itself from there, easily commanded to center on whatever point the screen personality preferred.

Live updates went into more than a hundred handheld machines, phones, and pads alike, updating the latest vote tallies from the primaries. Elsewhere in Northern Virginia, a party honored Senator Benjamin Pettus, who coasted to victory in his primary. Widely respected in the state party, no one officially declared their opposition. A few names were written in, some minute dissents within the confidentiality of the voting booth. Yet no one truly stood a chance. Indeed, for all the uplifting revelry of the opposition's rally, those in the know held little hope for their expected nominee.

Yet Vanessa Gutierrez was confident of victory. She was confident in a lot of things. It was a feature that pervaded her life. Gutierrez started out as the poor daughter of a Venezuelan political refugee who lost all for standing against socialism. She grew up working two jobs and then worked full-time while going to school full-time. Through it all, the missed leisure and the absent privilege, she remained confident. Something inside of her always led her to conclude that she would succeed. Given her string of successes— a bachelor of arts with honors, a high-paying corporate job, and a happy marriage with two kids—it was hard to dismiss her audacity as mere hubris.

Cheers and applause began to counter the music for auditory dominance. These longer and longer bouts of celebratory upheaval were generated by the twin forces of Gutierrez appearing on stage and updated results showing her with a clear lead. Screen reporters ordered their cameras to face them with the crowd, the stage, and the prominent folks on it in the background. They, too, had received the news. She was going to win. She was going to have the honor of being an underdog, to make political battle with the elder statesman himself, Senator Pettus.

Johnnie Bedford had wagered on the right horse. He had coordinated campaigns in hostile elections in the past. While his projects normally ended in failure, party leaders were impressed by the fact that some of them succeeded. Bedford believed that for a left-leaning Commonwealth like Virginia, there needed to be a young, working, minority, female candidate to battle the old, white, male incumbent. Bedford was on the stage with Gutierrez, her husband, and their small children. He touched the amplifier device stationed near the edge of the platform to begin speaking.

"Well," he said with a big smile. "I guess we all know who is going to be the next senator representing Virginia!" The latter half of his sentence, even with the microphonic aid, was covered by the cheering and elated screams. "Mrs. Vanessa Gutierrez is an amazing woman. A powerful businesswoman, a devoted wife, a loving mother, and a committed Christian. And she can crochet backwards." That last comment brought a moderate amount of light laughter, Gutierrez among those finding the quip amusing. "She has always been the unexpected. The unexpected straight-A college student. The unexpected hard-working employee who went from part-time customer service rep to assistant store manager. The unexpected investor and entrepreneur. And she will be THE UNEXPECTED WINNER this coming November!" Again the cheers competed with the amplified voice of Bedford for control of the sound waves. "So without further ado, I present to you Mrs. Vanessa Elena Guuuuuu-tierrez!"

"Thank you, thank you," the candidate said to the roaring crowd before her. She then briefly directed her attention to Bedford. "Thank you, Johnnie." He humbly nodded and stepped aside so that she could address the crowd with an amplified voice. The device attached to the stage, through complex computer programming, knew to focus the amplification on her. Meanwhile, the automated news cameras knew to zoom their lenses to Gutierrez. "We are here because we are sick, SICK, of the status quo. We are sick, SICK, of Washington, D.C. failing us and the rest of the country. And we are, sick, SICK of this ridiculous, ineffective, harmful, government-run healthcare!"

Andrew McClellan was left of the audience. He found the rhetoric of Gutierrez to be without substance, and he took comfort in knowing that her chances of victory were pretty bad. His preference would have been to avoid the event altogether and have the night off. However, his editor wanted more stories on minority women running for national office, and so he was stuck there. If possible, his editor wanted an interview from the candidate. Andrew had his questions ready, and his recording device was linked wirelessly to the platform amplifier, guaranteeing a near-perfect audio recording.

"I am running so that my two beautiful children can have a future with more freedom and less government bureaucracy. I am running to represent you, the voter, the hard-working American who deserves to keep more of YOUR MONEY when the paycheck comes," she continued, each line getting cheers and applause.

"Fancy meeting you here," declared Michael Chan, nearly causing Andrew to jump. *The Kensington Post* reporter had been so focused on the front of the meeting room that he had not paid attention to the approaching amateur reporter.

"Hi there, Mr. Citizen Journalist," quipped Andrew. "I'm surprised the whole building did not fall silent in homage when you entered."

"Maybe it did," he jokingly countered. "I mean, I've been here longer than you have."

"Really?"

"Been here since it started," Chan replied. "And I know you showed up about an hour later."

"Guilty."

"And I did my share of 'man on the street' interviews. Now I just need to interview the future senator from Virginia, Mrs. Gutierrez."

"Future senator, huh?" Andrew folded his arms with skeptical amusement. "I guess you citizen journalists aren't the least bit biased."

"I am honest about my biases," Chan countered. "How about you?"

"Regardless of who has more bias and which way said bias goes, the fact is I am in contact with her P.R. person, and he texted me saying that Gutierrez only has time for one interview tonight."

"Funny," said Chan. "Bedford told me the exact same thing."

"Sounds like a challenge."

"Well, let me just say that I am only too happy to let you sit in and take notes," said Chan, with an aura of inevitable victory. "And, if you talk nicely to me, I might even let you ask a question. But only one, as my time is precious."

"Sounds like you missed a great career in comedy, buddy-boy," replied Andrew, with a similar heightened sense of obvious eventual success. "I am a professional journalist representing a news publication that is nationally recognized, award-winning, and with about ten times the online traffic as your little site."

"Five times," accurately corrected Chan.

"Five or ten, the result is the same. My interview gives her a bigger audience. And politicians love bigger audiences."

"Your publication is liberally biased and will likely endorse her opponent . . . again. Why would she want to entertain a newspaper that she knows will actively work against her campaign?"

"Because she will be smart enough to know the difference between an editorial board and a news page. That's why."

Neither of the two noticed at first, but Bedford had gradually moved to the back of the platform and then descended a short staircase to leave while Gutierrez continued to speak. He knew that her remarks were going to be over soon. He also was aware of the multiple folks who had requested interviews with the newly chosen candidate. Chan looked over Andrew's shoulder when he first saw Bedford coming. The distracted gaze prompted Andrew to turn around.

"Hello, hello," Bedford said when approaching both men. He shook their hands and exchanged pleasantries. "Okay, just as I mentioned before, Gutierrez can only take one interview and a couple of questions. I thought she was going to include both of you, but apparently she just wants to speak to Mr. Chan."

Andrew was dumbfounded. Chan gave a smirk while walking by, remarking to his rival "I guess my citizen journalist presence silenced at least one person." Andrew gave a wry smile in return as Bedford and Chan walked toward the stage, the candidate's speech having just concluded.

. . . . . .

For Roberta Sheridan, the assignment felt a little weird. The story was fairly normal. Inflammatory, troubling, but normal. There was nothing peculiar about the details of the happening. Neither were the content of the interviews particularly strange. The interview she was conducting was being performed like so many before it, with her and the subject looking at each other via computer screen, with a recording device capturing all words and automatically transcribing them with ninety-nine percent accuracy. The process was normal, the technology typical of that age.

Yet Roberta felt strange talking to activist Clara Grant, the very woman whom she had interviewed some time ago for the article about Senator Benjamin Pettus. When she was given the assignment earlier that day, she wondered if the matter would be broached by her interviewee. She wondered if she should be the one to broach it. What a disappointing update, indeed. The investigative story was shelved, placed to the side because her editor found greater import among other developments in the world. Roberta kept it professional and focused on the immediate.

"I saw the vandalism with my own eyes," explained Grant. "When I took my grandchildren to class that morning. It was not something children should see. It was bad enough to have the letters broken and some pulled off the school wall. But to have such mean-spirited and, at times, profanity-laden comments was just wrong."

"So, to be clear, they hadn't covered up the damage yet?"

"We arrived very early. Both of them serve as patrols."

"Okay, I see," Roberta responded with a nod. "What is your opinion of the vandalism?"

"I do not condone such violence. We can be better at disagreeing than that," admitted Grant. "That said, it shows just how offensive and despicable the name Barack Obama is to a whole lot of people. I agree that while spray painting 'baby-killer' and profanities on the school wall was a bit much, at least some of that is true. As president, Obama was a baby-killer. While he never performed an abortion, he created a climate that encouraged the practice. Therefore, he should not be awarded honors like having his name plastered on our schools."

"So you will continue your effort to get the school board to change the name?"

"Yes," Grant stated firmly. "There are plenty of decent New Jerseyans who are more deserving of having his or her name on a school."

"All right, then," concluded Sheridan. "Thank you for getting back to me and answering my questions. I will be writing up the article momentarily. It should be on *The Kensington Post's* website by tomorrow morning."

"Thank you, Roberta," Grant responded. She paused and raised a finger to interrupt the disconnection process. "One more thing, how's the Pettus story coming along?"

"Well, off the record, of course," cautioned Roberta. "I am still working on it in my free time. My editor does not think it needs to be finished anytime soon."

"Okay, understood," said Grant, who added, "just so long as it gets finished before it is too late to make a difference."

"Yes."

"Have you contacted all those places I gave you?"

"Most of them. After I finish this story, I plan to contact the rest of them."

"Nothing yet, huh?"

"No."

"Well, let me know if you need any more help."

"Thank you."

"Bye."

Roberta and Grant each removed their connection to the other at about the same time. Sheridan tabled the topic in her mind as she focused on the immediate. Roberta had comments from both Grant and a representative of the school board. Both parties denounced the vandalism. Grant maintained a solid supporter of changing the name while the official was neutral. There were really no other parties. Roberta knew that many locals liked the name and felt it a matter of heritage. She knew that ordinary folks did not care enough to think that an extra effort should be made to rectify an issue that most did not believe warranted such a fuss. Roberta herself held no real position on the issue. It was not a debate that inflamed her spirit.

The article about the vandalized school name was written up with speed and efficiency. Roberta easily copied and pasted quotes from both interviews, as well as paraphrased some of their comments. She had two news articles that others working for *The Kensington Post* had published earlier, giving her ready access to properly simplified background information. Her tactic was to copy and paste the background information from her coworkers, then paraphrase here and there so as to convey the same information but in her words rather than theirs. The key was to make them sufficiently different to avoid accusations of internal plagiarism yet close enough that the meaning was the same.

"Submitted!" she informed Jocelyn Lopez via the internal instant chat system. Her editor sent a quick reply confirming things on her end.

Roberta leaned back into her office chair. She felt the need for a few minutes of respite before going onto the next assignment. She knew that her editor could interrupt through instant chat, asking for a clarification or something that required a face-to-face meeting. Rarely did the latter occur. It was the early afternoon, when she normally completed her daily work. Usually, this time was divided between searching for story ideas to pitch the following morning and fraternizing with coworkers. Or a rest of a conscious kind. Roberta had a few pitches listed for the following day.

Getting back to a professional posture, she returned to that long-term project. Her editor allowed her to continue working on it whenever Roberta felt the need or the inspiration to do so, provided other projects were done or awaiting a next step that was out of her hands. Roberta had a saved email draft that included various notes for assorted assignments. It was also where she listed her pitches and assignments for a given day. Clicking on the draft opened it and displayed names of plastic surgery businesses. Of the twenty-three companies listed, all but three were crossed out.

Long before Roberta became a journalist, the action of contacting a facility for the medical records of a person without their consent normally ran afoul of the Health Insurance Portability and Accountability Act. Only in rare circumstances could someone access such information legally, such as a police investigation. However, with the information chaos created by the Ultralord Virus, lawmakers and others concluded that HIPAA had to be amended. Changes approved to the law included allowing general access to medical records for public figures who had been a missing person for at least twenty years or a citizen in general who had been declared dead following a period of being a missing person for over ten years.

Roberta opted to use the voice-only calling system on her computer, concluding that a visual cue was unnecessary for this research. She punched in the number, with the phone ringing a few rounds before a woman picked up. "Ventura Cosmetic and Plastic Surgery Specialists, how may I help you?"

"Hello, my name is Roberta Sheridan, and I am a reporter with *The Kensington Post*. I am doing research for a news story, and I was wondering if you could look up something in your records."

"Sure! What do you need to know?"

"Well, it will sound a little weird, but I need to know if your business ever had Edgar Hood as a patient."

"The American Mengele?" asked the receptionist with incredulity.

"Yes, him. A source told me that he probably received major plastic surgery before he disappeared."

"Yes, I see. Makes sense," she responded. She returned to a normal tone of voice. "Well, let me check our archives real quick. Can you hold?"

"Yes. Thank you."

"Okay, one moment," the receptionist replied, cutting off a bit of the "t" sound from "moment" as she put Roberta on hold. Synthesizer music came onto the phone, with Roberta waiting on the line. No new questions from her editor about the submitted story. Everything appeared to be going normally with that assignment. She was beginning to consider looking into doing something to pass the hold time when the public domain sounds halted and the receptionist spoke up. "Are you still there?"

"Yes."

"Okay, so I checked our records and we have no evidence that Dr. Hood ever came to us for any of our services."

"Okay, thank you."

"Anything else I can help you with?"

"No, that is all. Thank you." The conversation ended. With a digital pen, Sheridan crossed out the business on her screen. She looked down the list and found the next entity to query. A dial of the number, a faceless call, and a series of rings ended by a person who picked up the phone.

"Hello, Johnson and Jacob Surgery Center, how can I help you?"

"Hello there. My name is Roberta Sheridan, and I am a reporter with *The Kensington Post*. I was contacting you about a story I am working on about Dr. Edgar Hood, the infamous American Mengele. A source told me that Dr. Hood may have had plastic surgery, so I am querying places that might have done the procedure. So with that, could you please check your records to see if he was a patient at one time?"

"Edgar Hood, you say?"

"Yes."

"Okay, I can look into that. It's going to take a while, though, because we only have hard copy files from that time period."

"Fair enough," conceded Sheridan. "Do you know when you can get back to me?"

"Later this afternoon."

"Okay, thank you, talk to you soon."

"Thank you, bye."

A possibility. Roberta was cautiously optimistic. If nothing else, she was coming down to the last possible places that Grant gave her information on that Hood could have visited for treatment. Roberta had called up another one of the last three earlier that week. It had been several days, so she felt no qualms with calling them again. Their secretary had said that they should have an answer by then, anyway. Roberta located the number, punched it in, and then made the call.

"Greater Ventura Cosmetic Surgery Center, how may I direct your call?"

"The office of Mrs. Harriet, please."

"One moment."

Simple hold music, sounding little different from the synthesizer tune from a previous call. Then it was cut off for a ringing noise, which was quickly stopped when the office person answered the phone. "Mrs. Harriet of Greater Ventura."

"Hello, Mrs. Harriet. This is Miss Sheridan from *The Kensington Post*. I called earlier this week about a story—"

"Oh, yes, yes, of course," the center representative interjected. "I have been meaning to contact you."

"Okay."

"Unfortunately," Harriet began, dampening Roberta's initial hopes, "we looked all over our records and found no evidence that Hood ever came here. Sorry."

"That's okay. Thank you for letting me know," Roberta professionally stated. "Have a good weekend."

"You, too! Bye!"

Another half hour went by without a phone call. Roberta continued to wait for the return call from Johnson and Jacob. She wondered if her shift would end before they got back to her. She considered calling back to give her mobile phone number, but then decided to hold off until she was nearly out the door. They were all in California, so their work day was still a few hours from ending. Roberta divided the leisure period between respite and searching for more pitches. Two more got added to the list for the following morning. The end of her work day was getting closer.

"Counting down to freedom?" asked Andrew McClellan, prompting Roberta to turn around and see the fellow reporter leaning against her cubicle wall.

"Yeah. I'm wondering if a source is going to get back to me in time."

"Breaking news?"

"Investigative, so no real pressure."

"I see."

"By the way, did you ever get an interview with Gutierrez?"

McClellan rolled his eyes and took a deep breath.

"That must be a no."

"Yup," he responded. "She just does not want to talk to me. So Jocelyn put Suarez on the assignment, thinking that a 'La Raza solidarity' would ensue. Turns out she doesn't want to talk to Suarez, either."

"Oh, boy."

"What?"

"Sounds like I will be next."

"Most likely," stated McClellan. "Say, you're not prejudiced, are you?"

"Ha-ha," deadpanned Roberta. "It's just that, I would rather spend more time on this one investigative piece I am working on."

"Really? What's it about?"

Before Roberta could answer, her computer alerted her to a phone call. She turned to see that the office of Johnson and Jacob was calling. "I have to take this."

"Go ahead," said McClellan, who backed out of the cubicle and began to pace about while Sheridan answered the call.

"This is Sheridan of *The Kensington Post*. Johnson and Jacob, correct?"

"Yes, that's right," said a male voice. "I was told you called earlier to look into whether we did surgery on Edgar Hood."

"Yes, correct."

"Well, we didn't." Roberta felt deflated. "I keep track of our archives, digital and paper. We did not service anyone named Edgar Hood thirty to fifty years ago. There were five Hoods in the list, but all of them were women."

"Okay, thank you anyway."

"Bye."

A click and the phone call ended. Roberta gave a sigh as she looked at the list Grant had given her. It was a complete waste of time. McClellan walked forward, again leaning on the cubicle. "Bad news?"

"Technically, good news," said Roberta, coming to grips with things. "I now have more time to interview Gutierrez."

. . . . . .

"They are our best citizens; they are our sons and daughters, men and women in uniform who give so much so that the rest of us may be free," declared Senator Benjamin Pettus from the floor of the higher chamber. "When they return, as they do from our current overseas conflicts, it is our obligation to care for them."

Normally, Senator Pettus gave his remarks like many of those around him, with a physical copy of his written speech before him on the desk. However, he was resorting to what most did for public speaking in that era, which was to wear a small teleprompter that wrapped around his head with a thin cord and hung before his right eye like a monocle. The text scrolled upward slowly as he went through the words, pausing if need be per a small button located on the top of the frame.

"We must look after the wounded, both bearing physical and psychological injuries. We must bear the weight of their expenses for their needs. We must never, never, never return to the days when thousands of homeless veterans struggled to live, freezing to death in winter and succumbing to sunstroke in the summer sun. We as a society, we who look after all human beings from conception to death, know better."

Pettus was giving his speech in the evening, a powerful outdoor light making the American flag above the Capitol Dome visible to the public. A good portion of the desks situated on the carpeted flooring were empty. Senator Anwar Muhammed was one of the seated attendees, being near to his orator colleague. He was not feeling comfortable. It was not the rhetoric of the senator from Virginia, nor was it some physical illness. Anwar waited—patiently, quietly, reverently—for Pettus to complete his speech as others were making dinner plans.

"So, I am honored that this chamber can come together—liberals, moderates, and conservatives—bridging those heated divides to serve this common cause of charity. I commend both majority and minority leadership for their willingness to work on the bill to expand care for our warriors. It is a noble cause, and the least we can do for those who run into danger for our sake and for the sake of the country. And with my comments given and seeing the lateness of the hour, Mr. President, I would like to entertain a motion of recess until Thursday at noon."

"We have a motion and is there a second?" stoically inquired the vice president.

"Second," responded two senators.

"All in favor of the motion to recess until Thursday at noon, say aye."

A clear majority agreed.

"The ayes have it. Session is in recess until tomorrow at noon," concluded the vice president, lightly tapping her desk a few times with a piece of ivory.

With the announcement, the news cameras switched off; elected officials arose from their seats; and many, from senators to spectators, went for the nearest exits at a leisurely pace. The session had a mundane agenda. Legislative items of note were not particularly polarizing; neither were they newsworthy for most Americans. These were not the kind of things that trended or went viral on social media. They were regular things, typical governmental affairs. The kind of things that were rarely discussed on the campaign trail because so few would be driven to emotion by a stance one way or the other. These tended toward bipartisan support with little sense of tribal betrayal.

"How did I do?" Pettus asked Anwar as the former took off his head teleprompter, turned it off, and put it in his pocket.

"You did well," responded the younger senator. "And I might add, very timely with Memorial Day being only a couple of weeks away."

"I should have mentioned that in my speech."

"It wasn't necessary. Like I said, it was just fine."

"Glad to hear it," said Pettus. "So, dinner?"

"Sure," agreed Anwar as the two senators walked side-by-side toward one of the exits into the hall, Pettus briefly patting his colleague on the shoulder. "Benjamin, I need to ask you a favor."

"What kind of favor?"

"A political one."

"Do you have a bill you want me to co-sponsor?"

"No, I'm talking about the campaign trail."

The comment prompted Pettus to stop in the middle of the walk-way toward the exit, Anwar doing likewise. "What's the problem?"

"Things are looking tough. That Johnnie Bedford guy. Your rightwing buddy. He somehow found a popular first generation American Muslim to run against me this year. His name is Zuhdi Nagar. Navy veteran, college football star, and happily married with a wife and twin girls. Totally conservative and already well-known in my Paterson neighborhood. The perfect opponent."

"I really, really wish Bedford was on our side."

"Nagar has out-fundraised me, and he's getting some more wealthy backers."

"Money and identity politics. That's a powerful combination."

"It gets worse," began Anwar, who paused as a pair of aides walked passed the two to get to the exit. The two senators each took a step or two backward to allow for more space so that the young Capitol Hill workers were able to get by with ease. Once the traffic had gone by, the two elected officials each moved a step forward to better discuss things. "Like I said, it gets worse. Jersey got hit bad by the healthcare law. A lot of folks, especially in my neighborhood, have been getting hit with increased premiums, and thousands reported losing their preferred plans."

"You know these are minor hiccups."

"Yes, yes, I know, but the voters don't," replied Anwar with great concern. "I honestly think Nagar can beat me. Internal polling is telling me that right now, our numbers are within the margin of error. That's the first time I've ever had an opponent who was that close to my numbers."

"Okay, okay, calm down, calm down," said Pettus, with both hands raised with his palms facing his fellow senator. "What do I need to do to help?"

"Can you make some appearances on the campaign trail?"

"Anwar, listen," began Pettus. "I want to help, but you know I have a challenger of my own to deal with."

"Oh, come on, Benjamin, you know Gutierrez doesn't stand a chance against you. She'll get the same twenty to thirty percent of the electorate that thinks you can do nothing right, and that's it. She is no threat. I am the one who needs help."

"There is that."

"Besides, this isn't the early twenty-first century; you can take a rail from D.C. and get to Paterson in a half hour . . . forty minutes tops."

"Right again."

"So will you do it?"

Pettus took a breath. He did not like to be actively involved in non-Virginia races during election cycles in which he was up for re-election. During the second time his seat was up for contention, Pettus helped another progressive candidate who was running to unseat an opponent in Georgia. Pettus' challenger used his absence as "proof" that the Virginia politician did not really care about his constituents. The ad campaign harmed him a good deal, with his re-election only coming with a nine percent lead, the smallest margin he had in his entire political career.

"Oh, okay," he said, Anwar cracking a relief smile. "I will do it."

"Thank you, thank you!" said the younger senator, shaking Pettus' hand up and down.

"Just send me some dates for campaign stops, and I will check my calendar and see what is available."

"Great, thanks. Thank you so much."

"No need to repeat it."

"And in return, I will do everything I can to get re-elected."

"I would hope so," said Pettus as the two turned toward the exit. "With your struggle, that makes four seats that are in danger of being flipped, and all of them are held by us. All it takes is one seat to flip, and then next Congress, when a repeal bill goes before the Senate, it will be fifty-fifty with a pro-repeal Senate president to break the tie. I do not want that nightmare."

"Me, neither."

"A lot of vulnerable people cannot afford a single seat to be flipped. Now that I think of it, I feel like I should apologize for resisting your request for help."

"No need. I'm just glad you came around."

"Same here. This will be very trying."

"Well, with you helping me, my seat will be safe."

"And hopefully the other three will turn out well, too."

"Maybe you should make speeches there, too."

"Don't tempt me," Pettus replied with a smile as the two left the powerful chamber and turned left down the hall.

. . . . . .

Roberta was parked outside of the main conference center at Leslie Printice Washington National Airport. Her vehicle was stationed on the outer curb of the three lanes in front of the many doors leading into the center. The curb adjacent to hers featured the occasional shuttle from nearby hotels and other companies. The inner curb, the one most convenient for picking up arriving passengers, was well-occupied by taxis, both automated and human-driven. Competition still existed between the two options, with some taking solace in the statistically safer robotic driver, while others took greater comfort in having a fellow human being at the wheel. Even when it cost them a tip.

Roberta pushed a button located on her steering wheel that allowed for the side-view mirror to zoom in on the entrance so as to see what people were coming and going from the historic conference center. It was a new device only added to the models released within the past decade. It was comparable to the early twenty-first century device that some cars had allowing drivers to see a video of what was behind their vehicle to allow for backing out of a space without having to awkwardly crank a neck. Only this one stretched its video lens farther away, allowing for longer distance preparation.

It was the usual lot for several minutes. Tourists, vacationers, businessmen and businesswomen, all going somewhere. Some with corporate determination, others with retirement laxity. Most had luggage that wheeled itself, guided by a small device held by the owner—like a wireless leash that guided a doglike suitcase. The result was that elderly travelers rolled heavy bags with ease, and parents had more arms to carry little ones too tired to walk to the cab.

A couple of folks had robotic assistants with their items, a courtesy provided by Printice airport.

Finally, she saw Diana appear from the doors, her rolling luggage guided along by a small device she put in her purse. Diana was four years younger than Roberta, and even as adults, she remained several inches shorter. The two shared the same hair and eye color and a general facial resemblance typical of siblings. However, Diana was a shade lighter, causing her family to sometimes joke that she could "pass" for her mother's side. Roberta texted her at once to confirm her location in the outer curb. Diana quickly replied, confirming that she was coming. After texting, she carefully walked between two waiting taxis, both automated, and easily traversed the middle lane, which had no shuttles at that time. She smiled and waved at Roberta.

"Hey!" declared Roberta as Diana opened the backseat door.

"Hey," replied Diana.

"How was the flight?"

"It was good."

"Need help?"

"No, I got it," Diana responded, lifting the one suitcase into the back seat. After that, she closed that door and then opened the front passenger side door to get in. She fastened her seatbelt, with her left hand laid across her plump belly.

"Feeling okay?"

"Just the usual."

"I see," added Roberta, who typed in the destination where the two needed to go. She chose the option of an automatic driver, a common choice for the vast majority of human-driven vehicles. The machine estimated that they would arrive at the office in fifteen minutes. It helped that the arrival and the pickup took place in the middle of the workday, providing less highway traffic.

"So, no problems getting in?"

"No, security and all that was quick."

"I can see that. Reagan tends to be pretty good on that," commented Roberta, looking away from the front window as the car itself knew when to speed up, slow down, turn, or stay straight.

"Don't you mean Printice?"

"Whatever," said Roberta. "I still remember it being called Reagan."

"Yeah, like twenty years ago."

"You know, Grandma remembers when it was just National."

"Yeah," said Diana with a laugh, hand still upon her belly. "She called me yesterday and asked if I was coming in to National, and I was like, 'What are you talking about?'"

"At least the GPS knows what the place is."

"Definitely."

The sisters chatted about various idle matters, tacitly agreeing not to discuss the reason for Diana's trip. They had already cried and hugged over the matter, with Roberta giving consoling pity along with the rest of the family. The tears had already flowed, the sleepless evenings mostly gone. Diana lived in the District of Columbia's metropolitan area, having moved to the location two months earlier. Older sister Roberta had helped her find a one-bedroom apartment in Virginia. Diana worked for a national company, so they simply transferred her to one of their offices on the East Coast, in particular their office in Arlington. Everyone was very understanding in light of what happened.

"Almost there," commented Roberta as the two came within sight of the generic office building that included an OB-GYN practice tied to a local hospital. Roberta took control of the vehicle, turning off the automated driving system once they had come to a red light. Once it turned green, she turned into the parking lot for the office.

"Ugh, I can't believe I scheduled this stuff so close to the hearing," remarked Diana as the car came to a stop. Diana was coming back from the most recent round of official events. They were never pleasant trips, but they were always necessary. Whenever she felt that she lacked the strength to go back, Roberta and other family members were there to help her along. "What was I thinking?"

"You wanted to get it all over with at once."

"Maybe."

Leaving the suitcase inside the car, the two went to the building and took an elevator to the OB-GYN office. They arrived a few minutes before Diana's scheduled appointment. Roberta waited in the reception room while her younger sister went to the back to get her regular examination. Roberta checked assorted work items on her phone as she waited for Diana to be done. She also chatted with friends on social media, including Michael Chan, who had some rare downtime.

When Diana returned, her face was sullen and her temperament dour. It was a melancholy Roberta had hoped would be left at the airport. She finished the necessary checkout with the receptionist before turning to her concerned older sister. "What is it?"

"Can we talk about it in the car?"

"Sure," said Roberta, holding the office door open for Diana.

"The doctor said there was a problem with my baby," she finally stated once the automated driver kicked in and the car was backing out of the space. "He called it a 'severe fetal anomaly.' He said . . . " She paused to regain her composure. "He said that I would have to have surgery to save my baby."

"Surgery? When?"

"He scheduled it for July," said Diana, looking down. "According to him, the baby needs to develop a little more before he can correct the anomaly."

"So it is correctable?"

"Yes," Diana replied, fighting tears yet still letting out a brief laugh. "That's the only reason I haven't totally broken down. According to him, it should only take a few hours under the knife, so to speak."

"Well, that, at least, is good to hear."

"I'm just really scared, Roberta," she said, staring at her sister. "I haven't been this scared since I first had to testify in court."

"Diana, you will do just fine."

"Pray for me."

"I pray for you every day," said Roberta with a smile, eliciting a smile from her sister in response.

. . . . . .

Roberta saw Gutierrez working the room. It was not an official political function. Rather, it was a meeting of metropolitan area business owners. Everyone wore their professional best: ties, dresses, pantsuits, and collared jackets abounded. Servants with trays went through the ranks, their silver surfaces including finger foods and wine glasses, filled and emptied. Small, round tables were set up on one side of the room, with folks standing around them. Larger, rounded tables with chairs were placed on the other side of the meeting chamber, located inside a hotel.

Gutierrez was all smiles, schmoozing like the best of them. She knew many of the present entrepreneurial types by name. She was able to recall basic information about family, latest personal news, and recent ventures. They added to her knowledge with each brief, light exchange over tasty snacks and fermented liquid. For those unacquainted, digital business cards were exchanged by the light taps of smart phones. A shake of the hand, a small wave, and, in a few instances, a good hug, and all was done. From there, on to the next person of importance, a platonic speed-dating.

"Can I help you?" asked one of the help to the reporter. A woman around Roberta's age and size was manning the entrance to the meeting.

"I am here to interview Mrs. Gutierrez for a news story," said Roberta, lifting up her press pass, hung from the lanyard. This was the only accessory that contrasted her fashion with those in the room.

The help nodded. "Okay, I will let her know." The hotel employee had a mobile device that included the contact information of all the guests. She sent a quick text message to Gutierrez to inform her that Roberta had arrived. Looking into the room from the hallway, Sheridan was able to see Gutierrez at the moment she received the alert. She was caught midsentence but finished her point before looking down to check her phone. The candidate sent a short confirmation alert, a buzzing noise coming to the help's device. She looked back up, all smiles again, informing her company that she was needed elsewhere. Leaving the small group on good terms, she walked toward the entrance to the meeting room and soon was before the employee and the reporter.

"Mrs. Gutierrez, this reporter said she was here for an interview."

"She is, indeed," the candidate confirmed before turning to Roberta. "A pleasure to meet you, Miss Sheridan." The two shook hands. She focused back on the help. "Where would be a good place to speak in private?"

"If you go to the opposite side of the room, through the double doors, you will come to a back hallway with some couches," she responded, pointing with her right arm as she described the location.

"Okay, thank you," said Gutierrez, going back to Roberta. "Does that work for you?"

"Yes, thank you."

With a nod, Roberta entered the room and walked alongside Gutierrez, who finished the contents of the wine glass that she had never let go of since she got the alert. As they walked, she placed the glass onto the top of one of the taller, narrower tables. "Did you have to go far to come here?"

"Not really," responded Roberta. "The hotel is metro friendly."

"That's good," Gutierrez replied. "I had a feeling this would be better for you location-wise, though I guess it is a little late."

"No, no, I'll be okay."

"Vanessa!" shouted a portly fellow in a jacket and tie. Gutierrez turned and was friendly yet again.

"Hey, Bob!"

"Just wanted to say that I was on my way out and to say goodbye," he said, pausing. "Well, then, goodbye."

"Take care, Bob," she said with a nod, the man turning away after giving his remarks. "A longtime business acquaintance. We have done a lot of deals together."

"I see."

"Anyway, on to the interview?"

"Yes," affirmed Roberta as the two exited the networking meeting through the double doors and into the back hallway.

It was a quiet space. As the hotel employee correctly explained, there were a half-dozen couches placed against the wall, small mantles situated between each. It was the first part of the hotel Roberta had seen that lacked carpeting. Instead, the room had a simple, bare, white floor, with traces of skid marks from the pushing of various wheeled objects. They were the only ones there. Noises of human chatter were muted by the walls and shut doors. It was a decent place for recording a conversation, Roberta observed. The candidate and the reporter sat on opposite ends of the same couch. Roberta took one of the small square tables and placed it in front of the couch, putting her recorder on the surface.

"Well, I guess we can get started," said Gutierrez with a grin. "Fire away."

Roberta turned the recorder on and got out a pen and notepad, which included her prepared questions. "All right, then. My first question, a basic one, is why did you decide to run for public office?"

"I am glad you asked that question. I wanted to bring about positive change to my community. Not just ethnic community, of course, but also the business community. Here tonight, I was meeting with fellow business owners in the D.C. area. Many of the people I have talked to, that I am friends with, who I have done business with, have told me about how punitive the federal healthcare law is for them. It hurts their earnings; it hurts their ability to hire others. It just plain hurts. We need a better system in place. We need repeal so that we can start over again."

"So, the healthcare law is the big reason you entered politics?"

"It is the biggest. I have other things I want to accomplish while in the Senate. Making the most recent tax cuts permanent, removing harmful and excessive regulations. The things we need to make a better America." She paused for a moment, appeared to think, and then continued. "Yes, yes, I would say the big reason was healthcare."

"All right, then, and what is your personal opinion of Senator Benjamin Pettus?"

Gutierrez stayed quiet for a time. Not in anger nor in dumfounded status. She was being careful. "He seems to be a decent person, basically sane. He has, by all accounts, shown himself to be a good family man. However, his constant defense of the healthcare law shows that he does not know what he is doing. The American people need new leadership, new ideas, and a new approach to this issue."

"What will this 'new approach' look like?"

"Well," she said, clearly struggling. "There are, um, many ideas on the table. These will seek to mitigate the problems of the current law. The important point right now is to stop the bleeding. That is what the current federal law is doing. It is a bleeding wound, and repeal will close the wound. So like I said, many ideas on the table, but the biggest first step is to get the current law repealed."

"Okay," Roberta said, jotting a brief note. "Now, as you know, Senator Pettus' seat is widely considered by political experts to be a 'safe seat.' Early polling has you far behind Pettus, as was the case with many challengers before you. How do you plan to break the cycle of losses that your party has had against Pettus?"

"It will be many factors that bring down Senator Pettus in November," Gutierrez responded. "First of all, I believe Virginia voters are sick of all the problems that have come from the federal law. I think people want a change. They want reforms; they want new people in Congress. The establishment has tried and failed the American people over and over again. People are angry, and angry people vote. Secondly, I will devote all my waking hours to talking to voters. I will go to places past challengers have been too afraid to go to. I plan to knock on as many doors as possible. I plan to travel all over the Commonwealth, not just Northern Virginia. People will know me, and they will know I care. And third, I believe we don't have a choice. This is a very, very important election. Quite possibly the most important Senate election in our history. People want to be a part of history, and making history by electing me to unseat Pettus is perfect."

Roberta could tell that her interviewee was done making her point. "Thank you for taking the time to talk with me." Roberta turned off the recorder as the two rose up from the couch. "I will be writing the article tomorrow. It should be on *The Kensington Post's* website by Monday."

"Good, I like that," said Gutierrez in a welcoming tone. As Sheridan was putting the small table back between the couches, the candidate changed the topic. "Now that we're off the record, how is that story about Pettus being Dr. Hood coming along?"

Roberta nearly dropped the table at the query. Somehow, she kept control of the furniture piece when placing it back to its original location. "Fine. Still researching it. I haven't proven anything yet."

"Okay, I get it," Gutierrez added with assurance. "If you need any help, I told Mr. Chan that I was more than willing to give it."

"So, Mike told you about my—our—assignment?"

"He said he might need us to help spread the word, maybe even give some resources in researching it. I have to say, it is a very interesting story. Especially for someone like me who, as you know, is very behind in the polls."

"I can see why you would like the story to be true."

"Like I said, whatever I can do to help, just let me know."

"Of course."

. . . . . .

Michael Chan was patient this time. He waited in the hall outside of the Enemy of the People Club like a good guest. There was no "citizen journalist' argument made before the host, nor was there any taunting from those leaving the gathering spot. Roberta Sheridan came about ten minutes after he did. An issue had to be addressed. She wanted to speak of it then, but decided it was best to have as limited an unintended audience as possible. Michael was surprised that she requested a table at the corner. No windows. The host asked if she was sure, and she verified her sincerity.

Roberta wanted to get to the point immediately. A grievance had been within her since earlier that evening. Michael did not know going into the meetup that she was going to bear forth this lamentation. The owner of the Chan Worldwide News website had an issue of his own. A point of discontentment which he believed required the advice of someone from the opposite sex. As they waited for their drinks, Michael spoke about his recent problem, with Roberta calmly listening. She felt that her complaint could be put later on the evening agenda. Indeed, it might birth the end.

"And so, now Helen is avoiding me," Michael said, suppressing his frustration. "I don't understand why she is acting this way."

"Maybe it was something you said."

"But what, though?"

"Did she become distant after a conversation? Sounds like it."

"Yeah, I guess," said Michael. "But I have never said anything awful about her. I've never criticized her. I've never had a reason to."

"Sometimes . . . well . . . sometimes you can say something that was not meant to be an insult, but it gets taken that way. Maybe that happened."

"Like what, though?" asked Michael, the conversation put on hold as the wheeled machine came with their respective drinks. Their attention was halted as the top of the robot opened to give them access to their drinks, kept chilled. After both took hold of their respective glasses, the top closed, and the robot drove back to the kitchen.

"Well . . . one example I remember from my college years," began Roberta. "I dated this one guy who called me a—and I quote—'smart cookie.'"

"Okay."

"You see, he was trying to be nice. However, at the time I hadn't heard the phrase 'smart cookie.' I just heard 'cookie,' and I know what that can mean. I told him off. By the time I learned the context, it was too late."

"Wow," said Michael, sipping his drink before continuing. "Sounds like I should find this out before it's too late."

"Begin with an apology," stated Roberta.

"I will. I was planning to."

"Good."

"Maybe I should text her now."

"Call her," ordered Roberta. "But first, we need to discuss something else."

"I don't think I've ever called you a cookie, smart or otherwise."

"Something else."

"What else?"

"Our little project together."

"You mean the article?" asked Michael, answering the question in his mind. "Did you track down the plastic surgery place where Dr. Hood went?"

"No, not yet, this is something else."

"What else?"

Roberta took a breath and placed a strong gaze upon her friend. "Mike, you need to cut your ties to the Gutierrez campaign and fast."

"How come?"

"Ethics, my friend who cannot get admitted to this club without a member present. Ethics. And it is very unethical for you to be actively supporting the Gutierrez campaign while working on this article about Pettus."

"Why?"

"Why?" she said, tinged with outrage. "Because it shows a clear conflict of interest. If you help write a story whose result directly benefits you, that is wrong. It calls into question the legitimacy of your claims; it involves advancing your personal self. Politicians can be thrown into jail for doing similar."

"Berta, Berta, calm down," Michael replied. "It's not that bad. It's not like I gave money to Gutierrez."

"But you are officially connected to her campaign. I learned that you volunteered for her office, that she has you as one of her researchers. And she sees me as helping her opposition research. That's not going to work."

"But, Berta—"

"Mike, she goes. Either you quit her campaign, or else I drop this story."

Michael was about to say something, but he stopped himself. Her stare was getting to him. He thought again before finally speaking up. "You would do that, really?"

"Yes."

"All right then, I will text Gutierrez telling her that I cannot volunteer for her campaign anymore."

"And?"

"And what?"

"And tell her that we will not be seeking her campaign's help. This will be an independent investigation. No ties to any political party or conflicting interest. Got it?"

"Got it, Berta."

"The sooner you tell her, the better."

"One more question."

"What now?"

"Should I text Gutierrez first or call Helen first?" he asked with a smirk. Roberta smiled in relieved response.

"Probably your girlfriend first."

"I completely agree," said Michael, rising from his seat. "I'll be back in a few minutes. Don't forget to tell the front desk guy to let me back in."

"Of course," responded Roberta, who temporarily entertained the idea of doing the opposite, just to further teach her friend a lesson.

CHAPTER 6

JOHNNIE BEDFORD WAS IN POLITICS since the beginning. His father was a local elected official who traveled extensively with the whole family to stump speech. Even when his mother was pregnant with little Johnnie, the two both went on the trail, going by car, bus, or train. Plenty of photos and videos showed his mother, great with him, standing by her passionate husband. When he was a baby, the appearances continued. He was surprisingly docile at the campaign events. Later, his father told him that Johnnie's pudgy cheeks and adorable stares helped close the gender gap.

Johnnie stood by his father as a child, wearing the campaigns stickers with his clip-on tie. On the verge of his teenage years, he was reading political literature, rosters of legislatures, and viewing the online live streams of pundits right and left. For a time, he was able to name every governor in the country and nearly all the presidents. He always tripped up on the forgettable group between Ulysses Grant and Teddy Roosevelt. To no shock, he participated in the school debate team.

Teenage years involved a greater and more direct involvement in the process. No longer was Johnnie just a cute stage prop or a biological encyclopedia of political trivia. He volunteered for his father's campaign this time, knocking on doors and placing literature on thousands of parked cars. He boasted of wearing out two pairs of sneakers during the months-long campaign season, a sacrifice that was worth it when the senior Bedford won re-election to his seat.

College years saw him rise up in the ranks of activism. Years of field work led him to become a coordinator of up-and-coming activists. Now other people got to wear out their sneakers. For the typical candidate, his work was divided between office and the streets. In the office, he spent all day contacting people, press, volunteers, potential donors, eventual donors, and opposition research experts. On the streets, he led the pack, dropping off campaign literature, seeing how volunteers were doing, returning to his old practice of door-knocking, and other miscellaneous acts.

Johnnie knew how to find people. He was adept at the research, analyzing each congressional district and Senate seat. Demographics, like ethnicity, generation, religion, culture, and all else. The variables were always shifting around in his mind, coming together to help him help local party chapters get the best people to run. Sometimes, the list of planned candidates was sufficient; other times, he had to find people himself. Usually, they were upstanding citizens, people who lacked experience but compensated with general admiration from their peers. People who would be hard to beat.

Ironically, it was a defeat that led many local campaigns to want his services. In Virginia, the Eighth Congressional District had long been a liberal stronghold. It was also the area where Senator Benjamin Pettus lived. Local conservatives sought out Johnnie for assistance when another power player quit over a family illness. Johnnie found a local businessman and person of color who largely agreed with the platform. He spent long hours campaigning on behalf of the opposition candidate, coaching him for the debate, helping to distribute literature, and doing the research for the attack ads. On election night, the incumbent prevailed by only a few hundred votes. Johnnie was in pain over the loss, but only briefly. The close margin in a district once thought impossible to gain led other campaigns to seek his counsel.

Johnnie became a specialist in getting people elected to seats thought impossible. On two occasions, his efforts produced national headlines. Other efforts, while not as memorable to the mainstream American mind, still paid out in success. The House of Representatives leadership credited Johnnie with aiding their takeover of the lower house. Senate leadership was banking on him doing the same for them. Johnnie committed himself to two races, one in Virginia and another in New Jersey. The latter was viewed as quite competitive while the former was the longshot.

Although that morning Richmond experienced a heavy downpour, by afternoon, the landscape was drying. Byrd Park was full of locals gearing up for fireworks. They came with towels and lawn chairs, balls for playing, lotion and sunglasses for the beaming sun, phones for taking video and photos, and money for the vendors. Many brought miniature American flags, many for the amusement of the little ones. Food trucks were parked around the major congregating spaces, offering overpriced hot dogs, chicken, hamburgers, fries, funnel cake, ice cream, cotton candy, tacos, lemonade, bottled water, and sodas. Dozens of trash cans with wheels, black lids, and bright orange bodies were present for human use. Later on, three-foot-tall wheeled robots with mechanical arms would roam the park picking up that which did not get to the proper disposal unit.

Despite the heat, Johnnie and his candidate were not sweating. Like the other tables set up for local businesses, nonprofits, and political hopefuls, the Gutierrez for Senate campaign table had built-in climate control for up to ten feet in all directions. Older models, which a few of the groups had, only went as far as five feet. The candidate herself was in attendance, interacting with each person who went by. She asked if they were registered to vote, answered all the rational questions, received positive feedback, took selfies and regular photos, shook hands, greeted children, got contact information for the list serv, and directed some folks to her volunteers, who helped to register for voting or sign them up for active involvement in the campaign.

More and more of the crowds were headed toward the Dogwood Dell Amphitheater, a symphony and a conductor present on the Ha'Penny Stage. They were beginning the lengthy musical agenda for the patriotic evening, beginning with memorable movie music from films released in both the present century and the previous. With the pedestrian flow turning to a trickle, Vanessa Gutierrez felt it acceptable to take a break. She went behind the table, going toward a large temporary cooling station for those working the event. Johnnie was already there, finishing off a bottled water in a corner.

"May I join you?" she asked.

"By all means." The two sat opposite each other.

"How am I doing?"

"You are doing amazing. People like you. And I counted about a hundred names added to the list serv. That's growth, that's a movement."

"You are good at building people up, Johnnie," Vanessa began. "You are a great source of encouragement. No question. However, I am a realist. I can imagine that Senator Pettus had a hundred times more people on his list serv."

"Possibly."

"I do not think that I will fail to gain momentum. I do not think that I will fail to increase my support. I fear that I will fail to make these gains and increases large enough by election day. That is what I am concerned about."

"Just remember, Vanessa, we still have four months before election day. And we have two and a half months before the big debate."

"Any ideas to level the polls?"

"Level the polls?"

"You know, drop his numbers."

"You mean attack ads?" asked Johnnie, getting a nod in response. "Well, we both know what Chan and his friend at *The Post* are working on."

"Yes, we do."

"I'm thinking a trial run. Something for only blogs and social media. Not the full blast, just a little bit of what we have. See what happens."

"Why not put it all out there?"

"We'll see. I am not ruling that out. However, it is best to hurl such a fearsome blow mere weeks before the election."

"The 'October Surprise' strategy?"

"Exactly."

"So, when do we do it?"

"Let's wait a few days. Let everyone celebrate Independence Day in peace."

. . . . . .

Roberta Sheridan had to guard against flying bugs that morning. The biters, the stingers, and the ones who perceived her ears to be flowers. The market included portable bug zappers that drove 99.9 percent of mini-beasts away from a person who wore one. However, Roberta had run out of the single-use products and had forgotten to get more when grocery shopping. It was going to be part of a special errand later that morning, when the temperature would be even hotter. Thick, District of Columbia air and a morning sun made it just tolerable. That was going to change within the first couple of miles. Good thing she brought plenty of sports liquid and dressed in her scantiest exercise shorts and sleeveless t-shirt. Her fashion was typical for those gathered.

Gathering with the fifty to sixty at the park minutes before they went on their intricate routes was enjoyable. Catching up with folks she had not seen since the week before, learning about family vacations, hearing updates on improving injuries. Also of benefit was that other people had remembered to bring their portable zappers, creating a large outdoor network of bug protection. A few minutes before the start time, Barbara showed up, wearing the knee brace she had been sporting for the past month.

"Hey, Barb!" said Roberta while waving. Her friend waved back and smiled, putting pep in her step to get to Roberta quicker.

"Morning, Roberta."

"How's the knee?"

"Getting better, just like last week."

"When's the brace coming off?"

"A few more weeks, maybe. And then I'll do the longer routes again."

"Yeah."

"Like I said, if you would rather do the six-miler, I'm okay with that."

"No, no, we stick together," Roberta replied, patting her friend on the back. "You keep me honest on my speed."

"Under nine minutes today?"

"If you're up for it."

Barbara looked at her brace and then looked back to Roberta. "I'm good."

"And so's the knee, I suspect."

"Yeah," responded Barbara, with further conversation being halted by the shouts of Joey, one of the organizers. He was wearing tight shorts and a tight jersey. Joey had shaved his beard as the weather became consistently hot. He still received his share of jokes about being a different person.

"We have three routes this morning: a six-miler, a ten-miler, and a modified eight-miler. As a reminder, for the eight-mile route, you follow the ten up until you get on Cardozo. Unlike the folks doing the ten, you turn back immediately. Now how many of you all are doing the six?" A dozen hands went up, including Barbara and Roberta. "How many are doing the ten?" Thirty folks raised their hands, Joey among them. "And how many of you are doing the eight?" The rest raised arms. "Okay, then. There is a SAG stationed at the intersection of U Street and Sixteenth and another at McMillan Drive by Howard University. You ten-milers are going to go by both; I believe everyone else will only go by one. As always, Abby will be out there. Rita and Baker will be at the Howard one." There were nods and thumbs ups in response. "Okay, then. Let's go out and have a good run!"

"Here we go," said Barbara as she and Roberta joined the walking group which gradually converted to running. Watches and phones kept track of each runner's mileage and time. Most of them used sports drink patches attached to their arms or some cases, legs. It did not take long for most of them to need to consume the fluids as they perspired under the early sun of the summer morning.

"Car up!" shouted Roberta when she saw a dark blue SUV turn onto their street a few blocks ahead. Each of the runners taking that route recognized the warning and either shifted to the edge of the road or went onto the adjacent sidewalk. Roberta filed behind Barbara as the vehicle got closer. Once the car passed, she went a little faster to get to her previous position running alongside her friend.

"And so, you're going to meet the person behind the Ultralord Virus?"

"Yeah," replied Roberta. "Pretty cool, huh?

"So, they finally approved the interview?"

"Yes."

"Wow, that took them a long time," noted Barbara, double-checking her route instructions on her watch as Roberta nodded in the affirmative.

"Yes, they had to do a big background check on me to make sure I had no personal connection to her. And then, they checked my media credentials, my criminal record—"

"Which doesn't exist, right?" said Barbara with a panting smile.

"Yeah, right," laughed Roberta between breaths. "So they had to check that. Then I had to agree to a specific date, which was hard because my editor wanted me to focus on a bunch of other stories. But now I'm caught up, so I get to go."

"It's like a field trip, isn't it?"

"It feels that way, yeah. I have to drive down to the Quantico area. More rural part of Virginia."

"My uncle calls it 'stereotypical Virginia.'"

"Yeah, basically," Roberta said. She soon noticed another automobile making its way onto their street from a minor road—a red compact that turned onto the road from the right side. "Car up!" She turned behind her to shout it directly at the runners behind her. Again, they got the message and pushed themselves to the edge and the sidewalks until the vehicle went by.

By the end of the jog, most of the folks were drenched in sweat. A few of the runners celebrated the completion of the exercise by taking bottles of sports drink or water left at the starting point and pouring their liquids upon themselves. Barbara and Roberta kept themselves under the nine-minute average, though the last mile was their slowest. "How about I give you a ride back to your place?"

"Sure, thanks, Barb," she said, patting her friend on the back.

Inside the vehicle, Barbara immediately turned on the climate control, providing the two women with a strong surge of pleasantly cold air. Special vents invented a few decades earlier allowed for the hot air to be sucked out while the car was parked without any need to lower a window. The trip back was much quicker than usual. Roberta thanked Barbara for the faster journey, and the two said their goodbyes. Soon after, Roberta was back in her place and made her way to the shower. She had set the device to a specific temperature, which it reached a few seconds after being turned on. The long, demanding run had the paradoxical effect of revving Roberta up for the day.

Breakfast eaten and final morning preparations done, Roberta turned on her laptop and immediately went to a news live stream. She planned to run some errands, including to get some more portable bug zappers. After that, she was going to chill out for a few hours before doing some housework. That evening, she was going to the movie theater with a few girlfriends she knew from church. Nothing particularly stressful was scheduled for that hot, humid Saturday. And then Roberta started watching the live stream, with the talking head giving breaking news.

"Is Senator Benjamin Pettus an abortionist? Several social media posts have alleged that the long-serving senator from Virginia was once an abortion practitioner, possibly a late-term provider out in California. Some have even insinuated that Pettus is actually the infamous Dr. Edgar Hood, commonly known as the American Mengele. The anonymous accounts who posted the allegations promise more evidence is coming soon . . . "

. . . . . .

Michael Chan used to ignore negative feedback. When his beloved Chan Worldwide News was launched four years ago, he received messages through social media and the official contact form on his website. Most were positive; some offered story ideas; and some were just plain vicious. Then came the correction messages. People pointing out the error in an article. A misspelling, a false statistic, a misquote, or a bad link. Sometimes, these valid complaints were buried in vitriolic rhetoric.

As head of the site and its sole editor, Michael had to look at them all. He bore the burden of seeing the problems and nitpicks. Because most of them were clothed in unfounded opinion or a minor glitch, Michael felt little need to correct them at first. However, this became a problem for follow-up stories. Michael found himself trying to build background information on stories whose specific errors he had forgotten. Other writers struggled to get good research, finding themselves having to rely on external sources for trustworthy information. Fewer embedded links to other parts of the website curbed hits, which hindered Michael's ability to fund his media enterprise.

So, Michael started taking these comments more seriously. He double-checked submissions, asked contributors for sources, fixed grammar errors, and issued correction statements when the mistake was just too big to downplay. Critics started to show more respect, expressing appreciation for Michael's new accountability endeavor. In return, Michael felt better for his project. He still received many negative messages and, even more annoying, publicly viewable blog posts and forum threads bashing his work. However, they represented a smaller percentage of the feedback.

The downside for this new professionalism was the loss of time. Michael was spending far more work hours analyzing submissions and fact-checking than before. Early on, he skimmed contributions. With accountability came a slower turnover. This was becoming a problem for stories that were time-sensitive. As Michael finally got to editing such an article and posting it to his website, it received few hits because the general reading audience had already read the information on more punctual news sites. Again, this threatened his ability to profit from monetized posts.

By that point, Michael had made sufficient earnings to justify hiring a pair of part-time editors and, later, a freelance copy editor. The two part-timers worked a few hours each day, dividing up the stories on the basis of subject. If necessary, one would cross genres to aid in editing should their focus have little work to correct. The freelancer worked in the middle of the week, either Tuesday through Thursday or Tuesday and Wednesday. Each of them had experience editing for mainstream newspapers, which helped with the professional aura of the work on the website.

Michael worked on his beloved website every day and sometimes during nights. He regularly checked work emails on his mobile device and made sure to never be more than thirty minutes away from any of his laptops. Despite the commitment, a typical evening passed with good sleep, and his physician reported no stress-related illnesses. On Saturday morning, he was checking over feedback that came overnight. Nothing particularly insulting nor troubling. Some compliments on reporting things other outlets were "too scared to report," a few scam artists asking him to invest in something or another, and a lone story idea that Michael felt was not worth covering.

Then his device rang. Michael was jarred from the buzzing noise. Rarely did people call him—even rarer on a weekend morning. He checked the screen and saw "Berta" written across it. He thought it would be a friendly call. A push of the button and the call began. "Morning, Berta."

"Mike, tell them to stop. Now!"

"I'm sorry?" asked a sincerely confused Michael.

"The Gutierrez campaign. They're posting stuff about our story," she said, exasperated and angered. "I told you to cut ties with them."

"I did; I did," he insisted. "So they posted about it?" Michael thought a moment. He opened a new tab and went to the Gutierrez campaign website. "That's odd; I don't see anything."

"It's been on the news streams."

"Oh, yeah, those. Are you sure that's the Gutierrez campaign, though? The streams said that the posts were anonymous."

"It wasn't you, was it?"

"No, of course not."

"And it wasn't me or my editor," Roberta replied. "There is only one other party that knows about our investigation, and that is Gutierrez. Mike, you have to tell them to hold off. And I mean now."

"Look, Berta," said Michael with skeptical calm. "Maybe this is a good thing. Maybe if they throw all the stuff they know about, it will lead other people—other sources, that is—to pop up and talk to us. There have to be other people who know about Pettus being Hood. Other people from his past and all that. It's like how decades back, women stepping forward with abuse claims against powerful men led to others telling their stories, which led to abusers being held accountable."

"Mike, you don't understand," began Roberta. "Etna Lee talked to me under the condition of anonymity. If certain donors to her pregnancy center find out that she used to work for an abortion clinic, they'll cut their funds. And who knows what other backlash she'll receive."

"Oh," he replied, confidence wounded.

"You have to tell them to stop. To not release any more information. Whatever they know is not going to help anyone."

"All right, all right. I will call Bedford and tell him what you told me. He'll probably want to speak to you directly."

"Sure. Just make sure they don't do anything else."

"I got it; I got it. Sorry, Berta."

"That's all right. Hopefully, nothing worse will happen."

. . . . . .

"Okay, okay, let's have that," began Johnnie Bedford, the "that" being another clumping of balloons red, white, and blue. "Yes, let's have that over there." The crewman nodded and planted the cluster of hovering helium-filled spheres near the podium. It was the last collection of balloons that the event organizer had to deal with. "And make sure that if any go flat, that you have others to take their place."

"Yes, sir."

"All right, carry on," he said. Johnnie got a brief nod from the crewman before both men turned to face different directions. With the campaign staffer, it was an issue of looking at other matters in preparation for the rally. There was still another hour before the doors opened to voters, constituents, donors, and others. He hastily walked toward a group of uniformed scouts, escorted by a pair of male mentors. "Welcome, welcome!"

"Hello, Mr. Bedford," responded the elder of the two uniformed men.

"Johnnie. Call me Johnnie," he said as he gave handshakes to both of the men. "I take it the trip here was not too bad."

"Easy traffic."

"Good, glad to hear it," said Johnnie, happily. With a hand on his shoulder and the other hand pointing off toward the podium, he continued. "Have your scouts go over there to the front. A woman named Tran will fill you in about what you are supposed to do."

"Thank you, um, Johnnie."

"You are getting good at this," he said, smiling as the man laughed. He waved them off as the adults and the youths, the tallest of whom was eighteen inches shorter than Johnnie, walked by in linear order, as though they were an elementary school class.

Johnnie had time to look around. Many people were around him. The troop that came for instructions on where to stand when the rally commenced, the color guard with rifles and banners, the professional singer warming up for the National Anthem, the crew dressed in casual black that was securing guard rails and testing electronic equipment, bodyguards at every entrance, and a few members of the press who came early. Johnnie found that one had even secured an interview with Zuhdi Nagar, the candidate he was working for. The reporter was with a local Islamic-centered publication.

Johnnie walked casually toward the senatorial candidate. While he was not close enough to catch every word, the exchange was clearly going well. Johnnie was able to glean such conclusions from the body language. The interviewee was not always so at ease with the journalists. He was shy, especially compared to Johnnie. As the campaign staffer got within twenty feet of the Senate-hopeful, the two figures stood up and shook hands. The Muslim reporter exited, checking his phone on the way out. Nagar turned to see Johnnie standing before him.

"How did it go?" asked Johnnie.

"I think it went well," Nagar responded. "He did not try to trap me like the last one."

"Good, I like it when they are well-behaved."

"I still feel a sting from that one. I mean, it was weird to have someone try and ruin me just because I am running for a conservative ticket."

"They exist," noted Johnnie. "Why else do you believe right-wingers have a history of mistrusting news media outlets? They skew left, and so they skew against us."

"It almost made me wonder if I had the strength to do something like this," recalled Nagar. "To have such critics waiting to pounce, to have such scrutiny constantly following me online and offline. Very unnerving."

"And yet here you are, still going strong," encouraged Johnnie. "Proof that an ordinary citizen can do extraordinary things."

"Extraordinary," repeated Nagar with a laugh. "I did not know asking people to vote for me was extraordinary."

"It is when you turn a seat that the liberals thought was safe into a battleground. That is impressive, and you should be proud."

"Pride can be a bad habit."

"Very true, very true."

"Still," Nagar added, "I am worried. I mean, what else are they going to throw at me? If I am such a danger, as you said, will it get worse?"

"Things can happen. My advice is to use whatever may come as more fuel to fire up your campaign. Show those sympathetic to you just how awful it is that they are doing this to you."

"Doing what?"

"Whatever it may be."

"I dread the 'it.'"

"Well, don't worry; worry never solved a political problem, and that's a fact."

"Anwar is friends with Senator Pettus," recalled Nagar. "What if Pettus gets involved, throws his weight, you know?"

"He might do that, but, inshallah," said Johnnie with a smile, amusing his Muslim acquaintance, "this should not be a problem."

"I know you are helping Pettus' opposition. Are you planning on keeping him busy with that campaign?"

"Let's just say I have something even more brilliant in mind."

"What would that be?"

Bedford's mobile phone went off. He took it out of his pocket and checked the identification. It was Vanessa Gutierrez, the apex of his other campaign pyramid. "I better take this. In the meantime, feel free to relax. We still have another hour before you need to speak."

"Salaam," Nagar stated as his ally walked off to answer the call.

"Hola, Señora Gutierrez? Como estas?"

"We have a problem."

"What sort of problem?" asked Johnnie, his smile weakening.

"Chan just called me, begging me to hold off on the Dr. Hood stuff."

"Really?"

"Yes, really," said Gutierrez. "I asked him what was the issue, and he responded that it was at the insistence of his reporter friend."

"And what did you say?"

"Well, I thought he made some valid points. So, I told him that I would talk to you," responded Gutierrez. "What do you think? Do we ditch the blog offensive?"

"Did Chan say who his 'reporter friend' was?"

"Yes. In fact, he encouraged me to contact her."

"I see."

"Would you like to talk to her?"

Bedford thought a moment. He was not convinced that the effort to attack Pettus' reputation with allegations of a nefarious past life should be abandoned. "You know, yes, I would like to talk to her. Maybe I can cool some heads and calm some nerves. Can you give me her contact info?"

"Sure."

. . . . . .

"I became aware of these baseless allegations on Saturday, along with the rest of the nation," began Senator Benjamin Pettus, his presence viewed through a small digital screen on a mobile device held by Roberta Sheridan. A cordless earpiece, wirelessly connected to the device, gave her perfect sound while she commuted on the metro train, her neighboring passengers unable to hear the speech. "And that is what they are: baseless. I have never in my entire life worked at an abortion clinic. Not when it was legal, not when it became illegal, and I will never do so even if it ever became legal again."

He was angry, yet tempered in his wrath. His fists were balling up, yet they never pounded on his podium. It was actually a pointless prop, since he had no notes from which to read. He wanted eye contact and gave it at every point. Roberta was not the only rider who was viewing it. Several news streams covered Senator Pettus' statement to the press, many devices seeing the same event from slightly different angles. She looked up from time to time to check her progress toward the stop.

"I repeat, I stress, and I reiterate that there is no evidence linking me to the murderous abortion industry of old. This is just another right-wing conspiracy theory meant to smear my reputation. They do this stuff all the time. You will be hard-pressed to find a liberal politician over the age of sixty who hasn't had these types of libelous accusations thrown at them. It is a cheap ploy to try and make my re-election race competitive. Nothing more. It is meant to divert away from the issues, especially the issue of giving quality health insurance to all Americans. This is the truth: Americans need good healthcare. Americans need a robust federal healthcare system. It is not perfect, but it is better than any alternative our conservative friends have proposed."

An automated voice announced that they were leaving Farragut North. Roberta took out the ear piece, put it onto the side of the device via magnetism, turned off the live stream, and got up from her seat, carefully walking along the moving car floor. Thirty seconds later, the transport arrived at DuPont Circle. Doors pulled open, and Roberta left with a small crowd of other commuters. They went by two larger groups of folk waiting on the platform on either flank. After they exited, these groups filed into the car, increasing the volume of those inside the fast-moving train.

Roberta went up the escalator, coming upon the great opening of the station. A beautiful blue sky with thin white clouds welcomed her and the others on the moving steps. On either side of the two aisles was thick vegetation that provided beauty and environmental improvement. Along the imposing circular stone wall was a quote from Walt Whitman: "Thus in silence in dreams' projections, Returning, resuming, I tread my way through the hospitals, The hurt and wounded I pacify with soothing hand, I sit by the restless all the dark night, some are so young, Some suffer so much, I recall the experience sweet and sad."

However, Roberta was not taking in this beauty, but rather rushed upward, saying "excuse me" here and there when going past those content with the speed of the escalator. She wanted the matter resolved quickly.

It was a quick pedestrian commute from the station to the fountain, where Johnnie Bedford had agreed to meet with her about "the situation." She felt that was the nicest way she could describe the matter. It was not a "disaster," a "fiasco," a "breach of trust," a "betrayal," a "failure," or anything like that. Merely, a "situation" and nothing more. She reminded herself as she saw the campaign staffer sitting on a bench facing the fountain that her story was not yet ruined, nor was her reputation. She was not mentioned by name, much less any of her sources.

Johnnie Bedford heard her walking toward him, her heels pounding the paved circular ground surrounding the water. He was punching away with both thumbs on the screen of his phone, a faint smile as he worked. Looking up, he saw a determined serious woman. His smile grew. "Roberta Sheridan with *The Post?*"

"Yes, Mr. Bedford."

"You can call me Johnnie," he said, still tapping away on the screen. "I will be with you very soon. I just need to finish this email." She was about to say something, but then he added a point of clarification. "Don't worry, it's not about your story. It's something else." The comment quelled her planned remark. Several more taps with the thumb tips and then the email was out. "Okay." He looked up. "Care to sit down?"

Roberta nodded and went past the seated Johnnie, choosing to sit a few feet away from the strategist on the same long, circular green bench. "As I said to Chan, I do not want anything else posted to the blogs."

"How come?"

"I explained that already."

"You did not explain it to me."

"Like I said," she added with a level of annoyance, "this is hurting my chances of writing a well-researched story."

"Or it is helping it, by opening up the chance that other people will step forward with evidence that Pettus is Dr. Hood. It is what you are trying to prove, right?"

"Listen, I am not trying to prove anything," she explained. "I am investigating a possible major story. I am still open to the possibility that I will not get any further evidence that Pettus and Hood are the same person. If this were a court of law, what I have now would not be enough to convict."

"You say so," replied Johnnie. "I found your evidence convincing enough."

"Chan showed you everything?"

"Yes."

"And you plan to post everything on social media soon?"

"Most likely," he said, then thought aloud. "Although, I am thinking of holding off for a few months. October surprises are a fun thing to do."

"I am telling you, do not do it," she firmly stated. "There is still a chance that Pettus is not Hood. And saying in print that he is if he is not is libel. All you are doing is making him the victim. No one is being swayed by this."

"Oh, that's what you think," said Johnnie, finger wagging as he used his mobile phone to bring up something to show the journalist.

"Here is a survey of recent major polls. Not internal polls mind you, not partisan polls, but scientific ones." Johnnie held the small screen closer to Roberta, who leaned in as Johnnie continued. "Since these allegations were first posted online, Pettus has declined an average of five percentage points. A couple polls put this decline as high as ten percent."

"This still puts Gutierrez far behind Pettus."

"True," he conceded, pulling the screen away, "but if just this little amount of allegation can cause that much damage, imagine putting out everything you and Chan have already found out, out there on the web."

"You wouldn't have a good enough case," she replied, "and you would be putting people who agree with you politically in danger of losing their jobs."

"Oh yes, the Lee matter. I guess you have me there. I can always make sure our bloggers are just told a pseudonym."

"Which will make it less believable."

"And coming from you, it will be more believable?" Johnnie skeptically asked. "How come? What do you have over me or my social media friends?"

"I am a professional journalist," she stated, then paused. "And . . . and to be honest, I truly hope I am wrong."

"Excuse me?" asked Johnnie, his smile gone for the first time since the talk began.

"What I tell you goes to no one but you, understood?"

"By all means."

"I like Senator Pettus. I like his healthcare law. When I interviewed your candidate about what she wanted to have in place of the current law, she could not give me a straight answer. When I look at the information on other campaign sites, including the Nagar campaign, I find a similar nothingness. You don't have a plan; you just hate his."

"We will figure out something when we take back the Senate."

"Knowing how Congress works, I doubt that will happen."

"Look, Miss Sheridan, we can argue about policies day and night. This city has a whole industry dedicated to making those arguments, left and right. But I will do everything I can to guarantee victory for both Nagar and Gutierrez." Just as she was about to raise an objection, Johnnie continued. "However, I am thinking you have a point. It would be better coming from you, and it would be better to have more conclusive evidence. I will tell our social media trolls to hold off."

"Thank you," she said with a breath.

"But if late October comes around and you still haven't done anything, well . . . like I said . . . I will do everything I can to get Nagar and Gutierrez elected."

. . . . . .

"The Lord is my light and my salvation, whom shall I fear? The Lord is the strength of my life, of whom shall I be afraid?" read Roberta to her sister.

Diana was laid out in a modern hospital bed, wearing a light blue Johnny gown and with a couple of tubes implanted into each arm. A sheet covered her body up to her chest, with her arms laying above the layer. Her belly was larger than when she first learned of the fetal anomaly, the bump clearly seen under the cover. Fat, white pillows were placed for support behind her head, neck, and upper back. She was calm and smiling as she looked at her sister reading from Psalm 27. Diana felt comfort from the words, as did Roberta to an extent. Adding to her peace was the earlier injection of anesthesia, made in preparation for the upcoming surgical procedure.

"Wait on the Lord," read Roberta, holding the Bible with one hand while gripping the hand of her younger sister with the other. "Be of good courage, and he shall strengthen thine heart. Wait, I say, on the Lord."

Diana nodded with approval at the reading of the Scripture. Roberta closed the Bible and put it on the table by the hospital bed. The two sisters prayed silently together, their words concluding moments before a human nurse arrived. Her uniform consisted of pants and a t-shirt, both a darker level of blue than the gown that Diana was wearing. She held a pad with digital information on the patient, confirming Diana's identity and the time of the operation. From there, she approached the patient and accessed a small, black box situated on the right side of the bed, just level to the top mattress. She opened the box with a key that only medical personnel at the hospital were allowed to carry. From there, she typed in a four-digit code on a small digital screen, selected the destination of the hospital bed, and then pressed enter.

After a few moments, the bed began to move on its own, much like the automated vehicles that were increasingly dominating the streets. It was a slow journey; the nurse did not select the emergency option. The bed successfully navigated the interior of the room, going by another bed that remained stationary. It turned into the hallway and then made its way toward the operating room. It slowed down when a wheelchair bound patient was being rolled ahead of it, only to go a little faster once that person turned into a room. All the while, Roberta walked on one side, holding Diana's hand and gently patting her belly where the main patient was present. The bed halted right in front of the double doors leading the operation room.

"This is as far as you can go," the nurse explained to Roberta, who accepted the news. "We have a viewing room over there if you want to watch."

"Sure, thank you," said Roberta to the nurse. She then looked down at Diana. "I'll be praying for you." Diana gave a thumbs up as the two family members parted company. Once the doors were opened, the bed continued to venture forth, stopping right where it needed to before a human surgeon, two human nurses, and two robotic aides. The artificial participants were not sentient, neither were they able to function outside of the parameters of whatever surgery they were present for. They were there for the precision cuts and mends, to confirm exact information on the current health of the patient, and so forth. Humans handled the other matters, once again fulfilling needs unmet by the cybernetic.

"Trust in the Lord; He will deliver you," whispered Roberta as she watched with patience and prayer during the course of the surgery. "Have faith in the Lord; He will see you through." Her little sister and her child were watched with prayerful angst. Amid her prayers, she kept thinking of those countless youthful memories between the two, playing in the backyard, spending hours dressing and redressing their dolls. She thought of all the stupid arguments and fights they had as teenagers. Yet she also saw herself as a protector, being the babysitter on many nights. In the present, she felt powerless at that time, just as she had in the past when Diana first called her and told her about the assault. Prayer and assurances of the competence of the hospital staff helped give her some peace.

Roberta watched with increased relief as the surgery went without problem. Her sister was completely unconscious for the procedure. A thin laser cut along her belly, and the unborn child was briefly exposed to the outside world. A sterilized, sheltered, interior outside world. One of the human nurses quickly administered an artificial "womb cover" as they were known as, a fairly recent invention that could successfully recreate the sensations of the womb while allowing a surgeon to operate on an unborn child. A robot was used to carefully cut along the chest for the procedure, with the human surgeon overseeing the finer details. As the OB-GYN had predicted, the necessary procedure to amend a life-threatening fetal anomaly was done with relative ease.

Within two hours, the preborn baby was effectively treated, and her tiny body was properly sewn up courtesy of a robotic precision device. While maintaining professional activity, inside the human personnel taking part in the procedure felt de-stressed as the hardest part of the process was completed. The head doctor was about to signal for the womb cover to be removed and the expectant mother to be closed up when the baby, with a reddish body, eyes closed, and a stoic countenance raised its thin arm and rested its hand upon the surgeon's index finger. It did not grip the digit, nor was any other conscious activity noticed. It may have even been an accident, an instinctive reflex.

He smiled behind his surgical mask, the tips of a grin seen by the others. Still smiling, he gently rested the fetal arm onto the chest of the little one, and then had the nurses remove the womb cover, close up the patient, and conclude the surgery. Diana remained unconscious but in stable condition. With the proper amount of sedative, nutrients, and antibiotics sent through the tubes into her body, she was sent to a room to recover, her baby in good health and developing as intended inside of her mother.

CHAPTER 7

SENATOR BENJAMIN PETTUS AND MRS. Vanessa Gutierrez met for the first time on the debate stage. Millions watched on local and national news streams on the internet, while thousands attended the event in person. A trio of respected national journalists moderated the nonviolent political conflict. The stage was Spartan in its décor, with a darkened background and simple podiums for the two candidates to use. Audience members remained off-camera and in the dark, abiding by the stated rule to make no reactions to the comments from the competitors. Pettus and Gutierrez were fully visible.

Civility marked the onset. Both contenders for the Senate seat walked upon the simple stage to the applause of the audience, their only permitted reaction for the debate. They each smiled and shook hands, exchanging brief greetings unheard through microphones. From there, they walked to their podiums on opposite sides. Each had a medium-sized mobile device with notes and statistics, so as to convey more accurate points in their debate. To prevent unfair advantages, the devices had their internet access turned off. Each candidate got three minutes to give introductory remarks. These were positive words.

However, the rhetoric battle was going to incur some figurative casualties, eventually. It began when the lead moderator brought up the summer headline-grabber. The question was actually directed toward Gutierrez. "Now, according to a third-party investigative report, the claims that Senator Pettus was an abortion provider before Roe v. Wade was overturned came from bloggers connected to your campaign. How do you respond to this report?"

"Well, first of all," began Gutierrez, "Let us not forget that the report in question was conducted at the behest of the Pettus campaign. The connections are out there and a matter of record. So, of course they are going to blame my campaign for the allegations. And yes, some of my allies and friends did spread word of the allegations on social media, but why not? Do you really believe if such credible allegations surfaced that I was an abortionist years ago that the Pettus campaign wouldn't do the same?"

"Moderator?" interrupted the senator, talking over Gutierrez. "Can I respond to that dishonest comment?"

"Dishonest?" Gutierrez bit back. "Is the truth dishonest?"

"Moderator?" asked Pettus, ignoring Gutierrez.

"Senator Pettus, you will get your response in a minute, after Mrs. Gutierrez has finished answering."

"Okay, moderator."

"Mrs. Gutierrez," said the stoic figure to the candidate, nodding.

"Thank you, moderator. As I was saying, we merely advanced the information we were getting from another source. A source not associated with our campaign . . . "

Roberta Sheridan flinched as she listened. She was at home in comfortable clothes. Her editor had assigned her the debate and agreed to let her work from home the following day in return for the late assignment. While Gutierrez was coasting between truth and fabrication, Roberta knew that the "source" she spoke of was technically her. For a brief moment, she wondered if Gutierrez was going to out her on the stage. However, to her relief, no such outing took place. A buzzer sounded midway through Gutierrez's final sentence, prompting her to stop and the moderator to let Pettus respond.

"As I have said over the past month, so I say again," stated the senator. "These allegations are baseless. To call them 'credible allegations' is almost slander. To promote them online is to promote something that borders on libel. No one here supports abortion. Not on this stage, not in the audience, and not among those watching from home. Calling people abortionists because of political disagreements is as counterproductive as calling people Nazis or racists or fascists. We need to go beyond these slanders and libels and focus on the broader issues. But my opponent and her allies don't want that. They do not want to focus on the issues, which is why they foment such ridiculous conspiracy theories."

His arrogant tone was getting to Roberta. It was the first time that she truly wanted her story to be published. He sounded so guilty, even as he made valid points. There was no strong evidence, only the testimony of two people who were pushing decades of memory and lacked solid proof. It was intuition, only intuition. A fiercely internal desire to reveal the monster behind the mask, the savage behind the philanthropist, the villain of the past behind the widely respected hero of the present. Roberta pondered these things, yet also paid attention to the unfolding discourse for the breaking story she was supposed to submit that night over the highly watched event.

"On to the next question," stated the lead moderator, turning to the veteran newscaster to his right, who provided the next query.

"Next year, the federal assault weapons ban will be up for renewal. Five years ago, when it was last up for a vote, the measure narrowly passed the Senate. Mrs. Gutierrez, if elected to the Senate, how will you vote on this ban and why?"

"I am glad you asked that question," she began. "I definitely stand in disagreement with Senator Pettus on this issue. Guns are an integral part of life for tens of millions of Americans. Further, we have a Second Amendment that specifically restricts the government's ability to control the sale and ownership of arms. Finally, while some have pointed to the ban's historic value when it was initiated, we must remember that the time period looks nothing like our own. When the ban was instituted, American society was far more violent than it presently is. Aside from the obvious—legalized abortion—there was also large numbers of graphically violent films and streaming programs, video games and virtual reality images that glorified vicious behavior, and a wave of internet-driven antisocial sentiments. We have since moved beyond all that, and so we do not need this ban, if we ever needed it in the first place."

"And, Senator Pettus?"

"Thank you, moderator." He took a breath of ease. Roberta felt he was relieved because they had moved past the abortionist allegations. "No one gets shot by a gun that is not there. A ban on assault weapons makes sure that certain guns are not there. Time and again our country has been without an assault weapons ban. During those dark periods, we always see a spike in mass shootings. My opponent is correct that our culture is more enlightened and less violent than it was way back in the early twenty-first century. However, society may change, but human nature does not. The ban saves lives. Every time it has come up for renewal, I have voted in favor. And I will do that again next year."

Roberta planned to include the exchange about the abortionist allegations in her story. Not only because of its popularity earlier that summer, but also due to its usefulness for background for her long-term story project. Roberta wanted to make it her lede. It was a hot topic, and other stories she and coworkers wrote on the matter were good hit-getters. Her editor wanted to know her ideas before she wrote her story. So she sent an email to Jocelyn Lopez, asking to do that lede. As the two candidates sparred over other issues, Roberta received an emailed response. Reading it annoyed her.

"Pass." A one-word death sentence for any story idea. No matter how much thought, no matter how much evidence, no matter how much she wanted to do a piece. From time to time, such ideas were simply destroyed with that one word of power and dread. Roberta felt compelled to appeal the decision. She fired off another email, asking her editor for an explanation for the rejection. All the while, Roberta kept an ear on the debate. They were discussing foreign policy. Pettus was making the argument that Gutierrez lacked sufficient experience; Gutierrez countered that her time as a business owner gave her plenty of background in negotiating with foreign figures.

"Still pass," replied Lopez via email. "Readers no longer interested. Find something else." Roberta knew when to quit, albeit grudgingly. Her coworker Andrew McClellan was braver than she and was known to argue extensively for stories he wanted to write. However, from what she could tell, McClellan had no higher a success rate on appeals than Roberta. Sometimes, she wondered if Lopez purposely said no to McClellan just to put him back in his proper place in the news publication hierarchy. Fortunately, the journalist soon had another lede idea from the debate for her editor.

"Mrs. Gutierrez," the moderator to the left of the lead inquisitor started to say, "regarding the federal healthcare law debate, you are running on a repeal platform. However, a recent report from the Congressional Budget Office found that repealing the entirety of the healthcare law would result in approximately three million Americans losing their access to medical coverage, including many presently battling severe illnesses. How do you respond to the latest report indicating that your position is dangerous to the American people?"

"First of all, consider the source," she responded, not convincing Roberta. "The CBO is a government entity. Of course, they will support a government program. Second of all, this loss of coverage would only be temporary. Private providers are the answer. They will swoop in and fill that void instantly. And third of all—"

"Excuse me, Mrs. Gutierrez," interjected the moderator. "But according to the CBO, currently, private insurers do not have the ability to—"

"Excuse me, I am speaking now," declared Gutierrez, getting some muffled reactions from the audience, who were supposed to stay mum during the debate. "And I am telling you, the CBO report is biased. This is America. We excel through free enterprise. Not government bureaucracy. Now, as I was saying . . . "

As she listened to the rest of the partisan rhetoric, Roberta shot off another email to her editor. This time the lede idea was the Gutierrez reply to the healthcare law and the CBO report. Roberta was getting concerned. The debate was scheduled to end soon, and Lopez had rejected three of her ledes already. Two minutes after the email was sent, her editor sent the desired laconic decision: "Go ahead."

. . . . . .

A member of the school board motioned to amend the agenda. The head of the board requested the specific proposal. It was under the category of old business. A motion was made to have Resolution B04 moved closer to the beginning. There was no debate over the motion; a second was given, and a vote was taken. Unanimous. Clara Grant, member of the audience, was happy to hear the accepted agenda amendment pass. It meant that the exclusive reason for her presence was to be addressed first. Nerves were not going to build up over the course of an otherwise-banal government meeting.

The stage for the monthly school board looked much as it did when Clara first came with her proposal for a name change to Barack Obama Elementary School. It had a simple black backdrop behind the board members, with neither intricate carvings nor historic pieces. The theater stage had large, dark blue curtains that were closed and three wooden folding tables placed end to end at which the members could sit. A banner was draped over the center table, giving the school district name and showing its prowling tiger logo. Two flags were positioned on opposite sides of the school board. A lone recorder was placed on the side of the table by the secretary, the device taking virtually perfect minutes.

The difference was in the house of the theater. Every seat was taken, and many stood along the back walls. Many more waited in the narthex outside of the indoor space. Several media outlets, many national in their scope, brought cameras and correspondents. Press alone occupied three rows of chairs. Parents and teenagers wore circular stickers upon their chests and bore signs in their hands with such slogans as "Change the Name," "Baby-killers Not Welcomed," and "Hate Not Heritage," a clear rebuttal to the minority of folks at the meeting who came with the opposite message in their signs and stickers.

"Before I entertain a motion to vote on Resolution B04, we will enter into a period of debate over the proposal," stoically explained the board president, slightly adjusting her hijab as she spoke. "Although gallery opinions were offered in the previous meeting when discussing the resolution in question, we will now entertain two final comments from the gallery. The first will come from Sam Pettigrew of the Save the Name Coalition."

Cameras automatically moved their lenses to direct their view to the aforementioned speaker. Hundreds of pairs of eyes did the same. They beheld a stout fellow with white hair and a gray mustache. He looked down as he approached the microphone placed in front of the board. Upon his person were two stickers, one for each side of his chest. The one on the left said "Heritage Not Hate" while the one on the right said "Save the Name." Upon getting to the podium, he took out a mobile phone and, with a couple of taps, brought up a brief speech he prepared for the board meeting.

"Members of the school board, my name is Sam Pettigrew. I am a proud graduate of Barack Obama Elementary School, a proud parent of a graduate of Barack Obama Elementary School, and the proud grandparent of a current student at Barack Obama Elementary School. Nothing about that name has ever harmed myself or my children or my grandchild. No one here can claim that they have suffered an injustice just because of the school's name. No one here can say that they were directly hurt by the man whose name is on the school wall. This board would be better served spending its time and resources to deal with actual harms afflicting our schools. Changing a name will not hinder drug use, nor put an end to gang violence, nor help any disadvantaged youth learn how to read. Keep the name, spend resources where they are needed, and do not bend to manufactured controversies. Thank you."

"Thank you, Mr. Pettigrew," said the board president as he stepped away from the podium and received a tiny smattering of applause. "And now, we will hear from Mrs. Clara Grant of the organization 'Change the Name.' Mrs. Grant."

Clara walked up to the podium. She was firm, convicted, and determined. She felt victory was drawing nigh after months of lobbying, petitioning, and holding the board accountable for their delays. Interviews with local and national media, debates with other members of the coalition, and rallies with thousands of students and parents in attendance had brought her to this moment. It was the same strategy she used in other jurisdictions to get other appellations replaced. Clara felt no need to alter a plan that worked nearly every time. She had no need to adjust things on the podium, even though she and Pettigrew were different sizes. The voice amplifiers had sufficient reach to properly project any voice in any room.

"Members of the school board, I have said a lot over the past few months. Tonight, I tell you only this: Our Supreme Court knows Obama's cause was evil. Our society knows Obama's cause was evil. History knows Obama's cause was evil. Act accordingly."

Hundreds cheered and applauded Clara as she turned away from the amplifier. Dozens raised their signs in solidarity, shaking them as though to make them beat with the heart of change. Clara waved at her supporters, giving a quick smirk at Pettigrew, who along with his few supporters sat in solemn silence. The board president tapped a gavel a half dozen times to cue the audience to quiet their passion. They obliged, with those who had seats taking them with hands and tongues kept in silence.

"With the gallery comments concluded," the president spoke in an objective demeanor, "we will now enter a period of debate among the members of the board." She paused. "Do any members of the board have any comments?"

"Mrs. President, may I speak?"

"Yes, Mr. al-Saleh."

"Mrs. President, my fellow board members, and all in attendance," he began. "I am an African-American. My people struggled for many generations to get this far in America. While I appreciate what Barack Obama did for my people, I cannot accept the fact that this somehow negates the many awful things he did while president. He helped one civil rights cause, but set back another. And another, when one recalls his many instances of cracking down on religious liberty. Surely, our state historians can find a better African-American figure from our past to honor in our school district. So, I urge my fellow board members to vote in favor of Resolution B04. Let us honor those who deserve to be honored, not nefarious politicians who longed to preserve a vanished world of yesterday where a human baby could be exterminated for any reason, right down to its skin color. I yield back."

"Thank you, Mr. al-Saleh," said the board president. "Any other board members care to speak in favor or against Resolution B04?" There was silence for several moments. "Okay, hearing no further comments on the proposed resolution, I will now introduce a motion to end debate. Do I have a second?"

"Second!" shouted three of the board members, roughly tying each other.

"All right, we will now vote on closing the debate on Resolution B04. All those in favor of closing debate on the resolution, say aye."

"Aye!" shouted all of the members, including the board president.

"And those opposed?" she asked, receiving no reply. "Okay, then." As she quickly adjusted her hijab again, the board president continued in a slower tone, to clarify what they were doing to the large audience in person and elsewhere. "We are now going to vote on Resolution B04, titled 'A Resolution to Change the Name of Barack Obama Elementary School.'" She paused. "All of those in favor of Resolution B04, please say aye."

"Aye!"

"All those opposed?"

Silence.

"Any abstentions?"

Silence, once more.

"All right then. Resolution B04 passes unanimously."

"Justice prevails!" shouted Clara above the many conversations and sporadic applause in response to the passage of the resolution.

. . . . . .

"'Justice Prevails!' New Jersey school district votes to drop 'Barack Obama' name from School," read the title typed by Roberta, who was seated in her cubicle at *The Kensington Post*. She continued: "A school district in New Jersey has voted unanimously to change the name of a school named after former President Barack Obama due to the historical figure's support for abortion." She then remembered the recent lecture about omitting has, have, and had from lede paragraphs, going back to delete the "has" from the sentence.

It was a quick write-up. Roberta had a transcript courtesy of the recorder from the meeting, as well as past articles for which to gather background information. In less than a half an hour, the article was submitted to the admin page for the publication. It awaited the editing of Jocelyn Lopez, though her editor was fairly quick. Only when other editors were on vacation and thus a greater workload was presented was Lopez less punctual. Sure enough, by the time Roberta had sent off queries to various sources regarding different news stories, the front page of *The Post's* website had the story prominently placed.

Her daily assignments out of the way or awaiting work on the other end, Roberta went into her longer-term project. Only a few cosmetic surgery places were left on her list. She never realized the sheer number of places whose chief mission was to permanently change a person's appearance. Many of them were knocked off of her list as soon as she learned they were launched years after Roe v. Wade was overturned. More were eliminated when she contacted them and they reported that neither Dr. Edgar Hood nor Senator Benjamin Pettus had been a customer. Some had been shuttered over the past forty years, making Roberta wonder if the business that performed the surgery was no more and her potential evidence had ceased to exist. It was an unnerving thought.

"We're sorry; we just checked our files, and no one named Edgar Hood received surgery from us during that time period."

"Okay, thanks for looking," said the demoralized reporter, again finding her search coming to naught. A press of the computer screen and the call was ended. She examined the list once again. A few of them asked her to call back or said that they would return comment soon. They never seemed to get back to her; she always had to remind them. Another business, another number, another call, and another confirmation of what she feared. No. Not here. Not according to their records. She found another one to call.

"Good morning, Premium Cosmetic Surgeons of Baltimore, Maryland, how may I direct your call?"

"Can I speak to Kelsey, please?" asked Roberta, who was making her fourth call to the business since June.

"One moment, I'll direct you," responded the secretary. There was a clicking noise, a brief spurt of classical music, and then a ring that was abruptly stopped.

"Hello, this is Kelsey."

"Hi, Kelsey, this is Roberta Sheridan with *The Kensington Post* again. You may remember I called you a month ago about my research story."

"Yes, yes, I remember," she began, then hesitated to add comment. Roberta knew less than desirable news was coming. "And I am sorry, but we are still dealing with archive issues."

"I thought you said it should be fixed soon."

"I know, I know, I really am sorry," she explained. "It's just that our company had to print everything out from back then because of the

Ultralord scare. And then a few years ago, a former employee messed things up. Until you called, we didn't really have a need to get things in order. It is taking us longer than we thought to fix the problem. Again, I have to say I am really sorry about the delay."

"When do you think you will have it fixed?"

"I honestly don't know. I'm sorry."

"Can you give me an estimate at least? A ballpark figure?"

"At least a couple more months, maybe more."

"That employee must have really done some damage."

"A lot," Kelsey explained. "Anyway, we will keep looking for it. If we find anything, I promise, promise, promise I will let you know."

"Thank you," said a sedate Sheridan. "Goodbye."

"Bye!"

For the rest of the day, Roberta focused on her more immediate assignments, those whose deadlines were more pressing and whose timeliness were more fragile. The drive to find the evidence on Dr. Hood's purported body modifications and his alleged masquerading as Senator Pettus was starting to influence the spirit of Roberta's work. As she wrote another article about the Pettus campaign, there was a dense disgust at the public figure. She had not proven that he was the "American Mengele," but she was starting to believe it in her gut. Every word he spoke about looking after the poor, every speech about helping all Americans, the value of human life, and the need to create a civilized society, all seemed to be despicable lies. A costume of righteousness worn by a foul demon.

"Roberta," said Lopez, who stood behind the reporter at the opening of her cubicle. The name-drop prompted Sheridan to swing her office chair around. "To confirm, you are going to see the Ultralord creator tomorrow, correct?"

"Yes," responded Roberta. "She is housed at a secure space in Central Virginia. I do not expect to make it to the office."

"Understood," nodded Lopez. "Make sure you send the science and tech reporters a copy of your interview. They would love to use it for stories of their own."

"Of course," replied Roberta, her editor silent and appearing to start to leave. "And I want to say again that I am grateful you are letting me do this on company time."

"Send your interview to science and tech and pay for your own gas, and everything will be square."

"Yes, ma'am."

. . . . . .

There was a small parking lot near the checkpoint to the property. On either side of the gateway was a large fence that surrounded the whole four-acre stretch of land. As with most sophisticated border fences of its day, the barrier had sensors that could identify whatever human being was drawing near and interpret the proper response. Guards and like-minded personnel were ignored, while potentially hostile individuals could expect an auditory warning to step away and then a nonlethal, yet temporarily paralyzing, electroshock for refusing to do so. A similar process existed for the lone prisoner. Approved visitors wore special badges that sent a signal to the fence sensors to ignore them.

Roberta Sheridan halted before the entrance to the building in obedience to the guard's raised hand. She had already been cleared by an earlier checkpoint, but required a final, more thorough processing before she was allowed to enter the enclosed space. Another guard approached Roberta, moving a handheld device up and down several inches in the air to confirm that no weapons were among her items. From there, she was led inside the small building beside the entrance into the fenced-in area. It was a plain interior, with white walls, a few simple cubicles, an American flag, and a portrait of the president.

"Please place all of your items onto the table," the guard formally ordered. Roberta obliged, placing her purse and press pass on the marble surface. Another uniformed figure came at the behest of the guard. She examined the contents of the purse, finding the recorder that Sheridan used for interviews.

"Does this have the ability to access the internet?" she inquired, holding the device in her hand as she spoke.

"Yes," Roberta replied.

"We will have to confiscate this recorder during your time here," she said. "We will provide you with a recorder that cannot access the internet."

"Okay," accepted the journalist, knowing she lacked an alternative. The examiner walked away from the table while the other guard simply stood in front of the purse and some of its removed contents. Roberta saw her go toward a small filing cabinet placed against the wall. She opened a drawer and got a rectangular recording device after a quick search. She then returned to the table to stand beside the other guard.

"You can record up to ninety-nine hours with this device. It does not have an automatic transcription processor. However, we will allow you to record whatever recording you make with your device once you return to this building. You cannot take our recorder off of the property. Do you agree to these terms?"

"Yes."

"The house is located exactly five hundred feet from the checkpoint, at a straight line, and should be visible once you enter the space. Do you require motorized assistance to access the house?"

"No, I should be okay walking."

"Very well," said the examiner, who nodded at her fellow guard. He turned to go to another filing cabinet placed against the wall behind them, opened a drawer, and took out a square badge on a lanyard. He handed it to Roberta as his associate continued. "This is a visitor pass for the facility. You must keep it on you at all times when you are outside of the house in case you get within fifty feet of the fence. By accepting this pass, you agree that you are liable for keeping it on your person in accordance with the rules I just laid out. When you are done with your visit, you will return it to this facility. Understood?"

"Yes," said Roberta as she put the lanyard over her neck. She also took hold of her pen and notepad, as well as the antiquarian recorder.

It was a sunny sojourn down the path toward the house. There were a few trees and a couple of stumps around the domicile, though all were at least twenty feet away from the structure. The house had red-painted walls, dark gray roofing, a front porch with awning, and a wooden fence for the backyard. Getting closer, Roberta heard some chopping noises. She was able to make out a person with gray hair moving in the rear of the house. As she moved nearer, she saw a well-built older woman with an ax, splitting logs. There was a pile of them a few feet to her left on the ground that were cut into smaller pieces. To her right were sections of a tree scheduled for splitting with the wooden-handled ax.

"Good morning," said Roberta, whose words led the older woman to stop her chore. She looked at the journalist and then looked down again. "I am Roberta Sheridan, a reporter with *The Kensington Post.* We have an interview scheduled for this morning."

"I remember, yes," said the woman, looking down. She removed a pair of work gloves from her hands, stuffed them between her belt and her jeans, and then walked over to the visitor, a hand outstretched. "I am Linda Harrison, and I made history."

"Nice to meet you," said Roberta as she shook hands with the interviewee.

"It's a nice place, isn't it?"

"It has a certain beauty to it, yes."

"Come on inside," welcomed Harrison, Roberta obliging. The wooden planks of the porch creaked under their weight. Harrison pulled open a screen door and then turned a knob to open a red-painted door. "Make yourself comfortable."

"Thank you."

"Would you like anything to drink? I still have some freshly squeezed orange juice from yesterday in the fridge."

"That's okay, but thank you."

Roberta was recalling a cabin that her family used to visit when she was a child. It was owned by her father's uncle. When he passed away, they sold it. The two places were not identical; he had sports trophies and paintings of nature hung over his walls. Yet the appeal was similar. They shared a common genre of wooden walls, a homely hearth in the living room, an early twenty-first century television, bunk beds in the guest rooms, and a large basement meant for storing hunted game and canned food.

"So you are here to interview me about my masterpiece, I assume."

Roberta concluded that Harrison meant the Ultralord Virus. "Yes. Let me know when you are okay with going on the record."

"We can start now," replied Harrison, holding a tall, plastic glass of orange juice as she sat down. She rarely made eye contact when speaking to Roberta.

"Okay, then, my first question, for background purposes," began the reporter, "why are you being held here rather than in a normal prison?"

"It was the condition of my punishment," said the infamous hacker. "The court said that in addition to serving life without parole, I could no longer be within two hundred feet of a device that could access the internet. Given how technological prisons are, that left authorities with few options. This place, however, works perfectly. Originally, it was a safe house for witness protection folk. To prevent bad guys from tracking a digital footprint, they built this place without any wireless access. No towers, no feed, no fiber optics. Nothing. Might as well be living in the 1960s."

"That sounds like a major change."

"Yes, it was," Harrison said and nodded, drinking a swig of orange juice before continuing. "When I first came here, it was painful. The detachment. All the disconnection. My first visitors were human rights activists who promised to sue the federal government, arguing that internet access was a constitutional right."

"Yeah, I think I remember learning about that case. I didn't realize that the Harrison of U.S. v. Harrison et al. was the same person who did the Ultralord Virus."

"Well, it was and is," she said, took another swig, and then continued. "By the time the case was in the Supreme Court, it was too late, if you may. I got used to this. It's actually quite liberating. Imprisoned for life in the middle of nowhere and I find it liberating. Outside air, only a little screen time on the television. Never having to worry about cyberbullying or responding to important emails. And now, I focus on my physical health and changing the physical world. I bet you didn't know that when I came here, the house had a gray paint job, and there was no fence in the back."

"I didn't know that."

"Projects. Projects like that. Exercise. Fresh air, like I said. It is all so much better than being stuck in front of a screen, punching away all day. Sometimes, I think we should all be that way."

"Wasn't that what you were trying to do with the Ultralord Virus?"

Harrison laughed. "My masterpiece. Yes, I heard that rumor. No, no, at the time, I very much liked being online. Just like everyone else. My reason for creating it was to make history." For the first time since the interview began, Harrison looked directly at Roberta, unnerving the reporter with her exactitude. "The Ultralord Virus was going to be my great contribution to the course of history. I had many reasons to want it unleashed upon the world, but they were all linked to that great human need to be remembered. No one will forget me. No one will not know of me. I am immortal."

"So, the legend that you did it to get back at a cheating boyfriend was not true?"

"Oh, no, that was one of the reasons," she clarified, looking back down and drinking from her glass. "It was the most immediate reason, but only one of many. A big one for me was that sense of equality. Do you know what I mean? Equality. A leveling. I liked the idea of leveling the world. Taking all that inequality and erasing it with something that would affect people regardless of their age, race, or sex." Her intense stare returned. "The virus is the most equal of all living things. Only the virus will attack without regards to one's identity. No matter how healthy or wealthy or privileged, no matter what you have done or have failed to do, the virus will treat you the same. No other living thing can claim that. To spread some equality always felt good, always does good.

"And that equality was spread via email, starting with my scumbag ex-boyfriend. It was very simple. Send an email with a code that alters a system's processor to automatically delete all content that a person has stored. Email it to an address. The new coding enters the digital system the moment the unassuming recipient opens the email. It then spreads to all systems connected to that one. Bank accounts, medical records, employers, the federal government even. Once it has filled every crevice, it finally enters the saved addresses of the recipient and goes out under the recipient's name. Even the suspicious person will open it out of curiosity. And the chain continues, spreading to millions and millions of people. That, Sheridan, is how you make history and advance equality."

"How did they catch you?" asked Roberta.

Harrison looked down and smiled. "FBI, their cyberterrorism unit, they were able to trace back the outbreak to my ex. When they realized that his girlfriend was pursuing an advanced degree in computer technology, well, all suspicion fell on me pretty quickly." She laughed again. "I can still remember how shocked the pundits were to find out that a woman did this. Everyone thought it was some nerdy teenage boy in his mother's basement. I bet even you thought I was a man at first."

Roberta nodded.

"Fun thing, this equality. Even with all the laws and the entertainment and all that trying to enforce it, we just instinctively draw up the same conclusions. And why not? I was one of the few girls enrolled in the CS department at my college. Meanwhile, the psychology department was almost entirely female. But I digress. My point is that I did an amazing thing. I did a historic thing. I leveled the unfair."

"Not to be too blunt," began Roberta, "but the Ultralord Virus did a lot of harm to a lot of people. Millions lost their jobs, their life savings, their healthcare. The economy practically collapsed; livelihoods were ruined. Many people lost important medical information that caused them increased illness. Some have argued that at least two hundred were indirectly killed by the damage from Ultralord."

Harrison took the criticism well, looking down, patiently waiting to respond. She drank the remainder of her orange juice, slow dregs sifting in the cup as she put it down on an adjacent mantle. "Yes, I admit that my masterpiece caused harm to some. But it helped others, many others. People who were in debt had those debts wiped away. Good people hindered by a past criminal record no longer had a record. Victims of online harassment were no longer able to be found by their predators. People trying to start all over got that chance." She stood up as she continued. "Almost every day, I get letters from people thanking me for what I did. Abuse victims no longer living in fear, families once in the red now in the black . . . " She blushed. "Even a few marriage proposals."

"It sounds like you are saying that some people purposely had their accounts infected with the Ultralord Virus."

"Oh, yes, many did," affirmed Harrison. "I get letters that say that. Some folks could tell that the odd random email from a friend or family member was my virus in disguise. But they also knew it was a way out. So they clicked and were liberated."

"Do any of the people who write you saying they used your virus to start a new life admit to being abortion providers?"

Harrison nodded. "I probably get more of those letters than any other. Nurses, doctors, other staff. Before my virus came, many of them were marked forever. No one would hire them; love interests would break up with them; bullies attacked them online and offline. Thanks to my masterpiece, though, they were able to start again. All the evidence linking them to their former lives was obliterated."

"Do you still have copies of these letters?"

"I keep every letter that is sent to me by my fans. And I always write back, unless they leave no address, then I can only do so much." Harrison walked over to a thin, wooden door near the stairway. "I store them downstairs. I even divided them up based on subject matter. The ex-abortionists have their own cabinet."

CHAPTER 8

RED, GREEN, YELLOW, AND AMBER leaves dominated the branches suspended all around the platform. No two trees had the same scheme of colors, with some sporting yellowy foliage, others reddish brown, still others a proper green. So many shades of so many hues. A large, well-trimmed, grassy surface was enclosed on four sides by paved walks and busy streets. Crisp air, mild breeze, and the warning of a storm threatened later that day. For that hour, the climate was welcoming, and the skies were clear.

The platform was situated in an area of the small park known for outdoor theater. An ordinance prevented a permanent stage for the sight. However, stage setup was quick and left little harm to the surrounding area. Advances in weight redistribution prevented scarring to the emerald surface, while mechanized joints allowed for the quick unfolding of the beams and elevated surface required for the speakers. The whole process took less than a half an hour for amateur crews. Cameras, both the privately owned manual hand-held ones and the automated hovering ones used by professionals, were ready.

Hundreds crowded into the clearing, some leaning upon or climbing the trees. Families came with little ones holding the hands of adults. Many descended from Middle Easterners came, with many of their women wearing hijabs or, at the least, dressing modestly. Other races and creeds were represented, ages varied as well. Soon came the pumped-in music, an eclectic mix of tunes, with patriotic, cultural, classic rock, classic hip-hop, and modern among them. Then came the presentation of the colors, the singing of the National Anthem by a local historical African-African church choir, an opening benediction, and then introductory remarks. Then, the presenter announced the special guest.

"And now, it is my pleasure to announce our first speaker, the distinguished senator from Virginia, Senator Benjamin Pettus!" declared the young man, shaking hands with the elder statesman as he got to the center of the platform where the microphone device was located. He received a strong ovation.

"Good morning, everyone!" he stated, getting several "good morning" responses from the audience. "Is everyone feeling good today?" More cheers, some yes declarations in the response. "That's good, that's excellent." He continued, several folks in the crowd taking photos and automated cameras recording and transcribing his every word. "I am here to introduce my friend and fellow Senator, Anwar Muhammed. Anwar is an excellent man, a devout Muslim, a loving father, a loving husband, and one amazing senator. Our Congress does best when it has people like Anwar in it."

Like many speakers of his day, Benjamin used a small teleprompter glass in front of one eye to show him the prepared speech. Muhammed was to speak after him and was planning on using a similar device with his remarks loaded into its memory. It allowed him to give more direct eye contact to the many gathered in front of him, his elevated positioning granting him the ability to see all who had come to the rally. Indeed, he was encouraged by the appearance of more supporters, trickling by the streets and into the lightly wooded park. He was passionate when making his next point.

"Muhammed cares about all of you—all Americans, in fact. He knows what I know, which is that our federal healthcare law is a necessary part of a civilized country," he stressed. "We are judged by how we look after our most vulnerable. Every society is. We cruelly judge the Antebellum Era for how they treated African-Americans . . . and rightly so. We cruelly judge the late twentieth and early twenty-first century for how they treated the unborn . . . and rightly so. If we repeal the federal healthcare law, then a future generation will judge us cruelly . . . and rightly so. Study after study . . . "

Benjamin paused for a moment, a brief hesitation of a only few moments. It was driven by the arrival of a few less-amicable attendees. On the edge of the park, standing on the sidewalk farthest from the platform, four people arrived. They held signs accusing Benjamin of being an abortionist. They wore clothes splashed with fake blood. He had encountered such protesters in past election cycles. Indeed, many of his fellow progressives had encountered the same; even one candidate who was born after Roe v. Wade was vanquished. Still, this time it felt a little worse, a little more threatening.

"Study after study," he stressed a second time, regaining his bearings. "Studies from many sources have shown that a repeal of the law would be disastrous for our country, especially for the less fortunate. The Congressional Budget Office just released a second report noting that as many as three million—yes, MILLION—people could lose their coverage and thus have their health substantially harmed. An independent study by researchers from multiple universities, also released within the past month, found that preventable diseases and dangerous illnesses will skyrocket should the law be repealed."

Like any experienced public speaker, Benjamin adapted to the presence of the protesters. There were only four of them, after all. And they were a thousand feet away. Contrasted with that small band was the grand, and still growing, throng before him of sympathizers and supporters. They sporadically applauded his comments; some cheered. The network of agreement was much stronger. "Anwar knows all of these things. He understands the importance of this election. He knows that we need senators who will reject repeal and in rejecting repeal, save the lives of millions of Americans!" That last line was nearly drowned out by the thunderous cheering and clapping. As they died down, Benjamin spoke up. "And so, it is with great pleasure for me to introduce my friend and fellow defender of the vulnerable and voice of the voiceless, New Jersey's own, Senator Anwar Muhammed!"

Muhammed came to his fellow senator, with the two hugging and shaking hands. Many photos were taken of that moment. Benjamin gave an instinctive pat on the shoulder as he walked to the side of the platform. Taking off the teleprompter glass and putting it away in his pocket, he reverently stood along with other minor speakers behind the younger Muhammed, who continued to rile up the crowd in support of his campaign. He applauded with the others, openly expressing his pleasure with what he heard. The incumbent paced around more when he spoke, but the sound system easily tracked his movement and effectively projected his voice outward to the mass before him.

Two more demonstrators joined the small group. Like the others, they had posters and clothes tarnished with pseudo-blood. Benjamin was getting a little worried. Thankfully, his senatorial colleague was betraying no evidence of being unnerved by the display. At least they were quiet and nonviolent, he thought. One of the newcomers unfolded a large poster held with both hands that, like his outfit, had large red stains on it. "Pettus=Baby-killer" read the sign. No one seemed to notice, being focused on the speaker on the elevated platform. Benjamin saw a few folks in the back turn to catch a glance, but then did little more. They were not buying the argument. In that, he felt some relief.

. . . . . .

Andrew McClellan and Roberta Sheridan patiently waited as Jocelyn Lopez finalized edits to a news article on the right computer screen. Her eyes betrayed no evidence that she knew two reporters were seated on the opposite side of the desk. A punch of the enter button and the article went live on the website. Jocelyn then turned her chair to face the other screen, typing up a few notes on an instant chat page with other editors. Her full attention went to the screen, again making not so much as a momentary glance at either McClellan or Sheridan. The editor completed the minor labor.

From there, she pushed a button on the keyboard above the screen, causing it to dematerialize. She shifted to face the other screen and pushed a button on that keyboard, likewise causing the screen to vanish. Only then did her eyes come to behold the two journalists she knew were accounted for in the office space. "All right then, now that everybody is back from Labor Day Weekend, I want to hear what you have for me. McClellan?"

He shifted in his seat, exchanging looks from his notes to the editor before him. "Well, my first story is a follow-up about the Smith scandal. Hackers dumped more documents online showing correspondence between himself and that Vegas showgirl. Juicy stuff. Maybe not family appropriate, but we're not a kids' publication, am I right?"

"You are right," confirmed Jocelyn. "And the last story got over thirty thousand hits in less than a day. So go ahead and look into it. If possible, get some perspectives from those involved."

"Oh, joy," he stated. "That means contacting Nelson, doesn't it?"

"I heard he can give reporters a bad time," acknowledged Jocelyn. "Still, he is Smith's spokesperson and is a big figure in his own right. If he causes trouble, direct him to me, and I'll remind him that it is against *Kensington Post* policy to let someone view an entire article before it is published."

"And that we don't get paid more if Smith looks bad?"

"Yes, that, too," said Lopez. "Anyway, I expect a detailed article. A lengthy piece that doesn't shy away from all that's going on. Remind people about the race and how he was leading in the polls against Senator Collins. Got it?"

"Yes."

"All right, then," continued Lopez, shifting to face Sheridan. "What do you have for me, Roberta?"

"I have two ideas. First, a lot of candidates, both incumbents and challengers, have been openly talking about pushing a bill that would offer reparations to Christian business owners and charity workers who were abused by the government in the early twenty-first century for opposing same-sex relationships."

"Really?" asked a surprised Jocelyn. "I knew that a previous bill was killed in committee on this issue. Is it the same bill?"

"No, in this case only people still alive from that time period who directly suffered as a result of state-sponsored attacks will be compensated. Though I believe the total is still expected to be pretty high, given how many businesses, schools, and hospitals were adversely impacted."

"Okay, okay, I like that. Sounds interesting," noted Jocelyn. "You should tie in the fact that Canada recently enacted a reparations program. Suarez wrote a piece a couple months ago about Trinity Western University getting several million dollars. So, that should give some good background, but ultimately focus on the U.S."

"Got it."

"And you had a second story idea?"

"Yes," began Sheridan. "I know we have not covered this a lot, but there was some talk among congressmen about cutting away more regulation to coil prices."

"I see," replied a curious editor. "Did your sources specify which regulations they were trying to remove?"

"I think it had to do with prices, but I can double-check."

"Let me think about that one. Summer is the big commuting time, so I am not sure our readers will care as much about slight increases for the stuff they put in their tanks, you know?"

"Yes," said Sheridan.

"Try and find out more; see how concrete it is. Keep track of it. Thanksgiving is in a couple of months. Maybe, just maybe, it can be an interesting story then, when so many folks are driving long distances."

"Definitely."

"Anyway, good ideas from you both," stated Jocelyn, who directed her attention toward Sheridan's coworker. "McClellan, you get to work on those queries. And I hope Nelson plays nice this time." He smirked, gave a faint salute, and then walked away. "Sheridan, I need to talk to you about another story."

Sheridan was initially confused. She was unaware of any drafts submitted to the admin page that were not already published. Then she knew what the talk was likely going to focus on. Sheridan decided to feign ignorance. "What is it?"

"It's about the Hood story," the editor said, waiting a moment until McClellan was out of sight. "I think we need to kill it."

"Kill it? Why?"

"It's stalled. We haven't gotten anything new for months now. While I looked the other way when you were working on it between assignments, I can't anymore. The midterms are weeks away, and I need you to cover tangible stories."

"Listen, Jocelyn, please," Sheridan began. "Mike and I are very close to proving that Senator Pettus and Dr. Hood are the same person. We can practically prove it now."

Jocelyn remained cautious and calm. "Roberta, you and Chan have had nearly nine months to prove this. If we weren't dealing with midterms, I wouldn't be asking you this. Honestly, though, I doubt it all myself. It still sounds like a crazy conspiracy theory."

"Jocelyn, you have to let Mike and me tell you all that we have; I am sure you will, at least, let me keep pursuing this."

"Roberta."

"Please."

Jocelyn thought about it, looking down at the desk. "Fine, you and Chan can come in later this week and try to convince me that this is worth more work."

"Thank you, Jocelyn, thank you," said Sheridan, who, while happy to make her case, still reserved some dread over having to make it.

. . . . . .

During the week, Roberta ran alone. There were running groups that met on weekdays; however, her commute time and preference for sleep did not allow her to join up. It was after she returned from the office that she went for a jog. There was a clear physical upside, giving her body exercise, strengthening lungs, heart, and legs. It also had a psychological benefit to it. Just to get home, be away from the screen, toss the proper clothing, don more comfortable wear, and then literally run away from it all.

Roberta was outside of her apartment complex. On her person was exercise clothing, sneakers, and a wristwatch to track her distance and speed. For longer runs, she included multiple sports drink patches bound to her arm. However, she was only planning to run a few miles and thus did not feel a need to hydrate while she ran. In advance of coming down to the outside, Roberta drank a moderate amount of a fruit punch-flavored sports drink. The weather was warm but overcast; a thunderstorm was predicted for that evening; and the ominous clouds were already amassing their troops for the attack.

"Trust in the Lord; He will deliver you," she mouthed under her breath. "Have faith in the Lord, and He will see you through." Her mantra continued for several steps, being as much a part of her preparations for jogging as the stretching. She got to the sidewalk along the street and from there kicked into motion. Her steps increased right as she pressed the button on her watch to begin tracking things. A walking sign along the first intersection granted her permission to go across the concrete route.

Despite the intensity of the initial spurt of the run, the bout of exercise was meant to be more leisurely. She was not planning to set any personal records. The rigors of the run, the pounding of the sidewalks and streets, the constant inhale and exhale, and the increased beating of the heart were offset by her thoughts. The distractions of the mind, especially pressing ones, aided in keeping her mind off of any agony from the jog. The thought of her editor shutting down her investigative piece hung heavy.

Roberta had adopted the faith of Etna Lee and Michael Chan, of Clara Grant and Johnnie Bedford. They all believed Senator Benjamin Pettus was Dr. Edgar Hood, the controversial "American Mengele" himself. Roberta felt that it was more than possible. She felt it whenever she saw him speak on the television. If she was the head of the Politics Department, the story would be almost published, rather than near death. To be sure, the evidence was mostly circumstantial. Yet many in the courts had been found guilty, even of capital crimes, when the evidence was only circumstantial.

The runner went a little over a mile and a half up the road before turning back. She had stayed on the left side of the road to be against traffic and went to the opposite side to keep the trend going. Ever since a few years ago when she trained for a 10k, she knew that it was optimum for a runner to not run with traffic. It was very important for safety reasons to be able to see the cars coming. Rarely did Roberta violate this rule, and this late afternoon was not going to be an exception.

A light turned green, prompting the runner to stop. Despite the shielding of clouds, the heat was getting to her. She glistened with sweat, and she breathed hard while waiting for permission to cross the road. She placed her hand on her neck, feeling a deep, throbbing sensation. Still, she was ready to conclude the journey. Apparently, the concerns about the meeting with Michael and Jocelyn were inspiring her to be faster. As though running the route quicker would somehow positively impact the future appointment.

She heard the first peal of distant thunder by the time she neared sight of her apartment complex. The next alert was from her watch, which informed her that she just completed her third mile. Content with the distance, she pushed a button ending the watch's monitoring of her jog and slowed to a walk. Again with the heavy breathing and the soreness with the limbs. Yet not beaten enough to keel over or to feel nauseous. As Roberta got within forty feet of her home, two things occurred. The first was that her breathing became normal; the second was that she saw Michael.

He was standing by her apartment complex's main entrance, protected by an awning. Another sound of thunder made him nervous. However, apprehension transformed into relief when he saw his perspiring acquaintance coming toward him. He smiled and waved, with Roberta returning the favor. She was expecting him to drop by sometime that evening; he was early. Roberta found no anger upon him as they exchanged verbal pleasantries; he must have known he was ahead in the agenda.

"Didn't I give you a key once?"

"Once," noted Michael, "but then when your brother moved to the area, you took it away so he could have one. And when he moved away two years ago, I never heard anything else."

"Well, I have a key," she assured, getting past her friend and to the door. She had held it in her hand during the run, gripping it tightly. When it appeared to be uncomfortable to do so during the run, she had tossed it into the other hand. She repeated the practice twice by the conclusion of the jog. "Did you have to wait long?"

"No, not long. A minute or two," said Michael as his friend opened the main entrance door and the two entered. "Can we take the elevator?"

"Sure," Roberta responded, changing her walk to veer that direction. She pushed the button for the lift, which came immediately. "We will need to coordinate what we tell Lopez."

"Will she be hard to convince?"

"Harder than me," explained Roberta as the two got inside of the elevator and the runner selected the correct floor.

"But you were eventually convinced, right?" asked Michael as the doors closed.

"Right."

. . . . . .

Diana Sheridan continued to push, her face pruning with each period of effort. Between each concerted attempt, she breathed several short breaths. The will returning and the muscles readying, she again labored on. Family watched from the adjacent room, with Roberta and her parents being in the delivery chamber itself. They gave encouragement and held her hands. A human nurse, a doctor, and two robotic aides oversaw the details of the process. Tubes inserted into Diana gave her proper dosages of pain-killer and antibiotic, adjusting slightly to comport with the proper needs of the labor.

After nearly twelve hours, and on the fourth great push by the mother, the baby finally became visible to those present. The crowning and then the crying, healthy screams from the little one punctuated the room. The doctor held the newborn up before Diana and the others. The umbilical cord was severed, and the flailing infant was placed on the mother's chest. Her breaths were still extensive, her body sweaty and sore. Still, just to look at the child, to feel her, to see her, to hear the congratulations gave great comfort. Learning that the newborn scored a five on the APGAR scale on both times she was tested was another relief.

Roberta had to take a break. She had been awake almost as long as her younger sister. She still had her press lanyard on, as she came to the hospital straight from work. Diana was giving in to sleep while her baby was placed in what was commonly called an "adaptation box" by her side. An invention from a generation ago, the box provided all the necessary health needs of a neonatal child without the need for wires or placement in a separate facility. She left the room where Diana and her child were resting to get some coffee. As she was nearing the room, she saw the doctor leaving. He recognized her from the group of family and smiled as she approached, curious of any news.

"Miss Sheridan, correct?"

"Yes, Diana's sister."

"I will tell you what I told your family," the doctor began. "Both Diana and the baby are doing well. The delivery went normal, especially for a first-time mother, and we expect both mother and child to be able to leave the hospital within a few days."

"Thank You, God," commented Roberta. "With the whole surgery before, I worried about there being complications."

"I wondered that myself. Thankfully, my colleague's work is exceptional."

"Yes," she responded, taking a swig of her coffee. Before the delivery, Diana decided to keep custody of the child and raise it with the willing help of her parents. "Did my sister give her child a name?"

"Leslie Printice Sheridan."

"Of course she would," noted Roberta. "She loves that movie from a few years ago."

"You mean Cutting the Butcher's Knife?"

"That's the one."

"Yes." The doctor nodded as Roberta took another drink. "Ever since that film came out, I have seen a lot of children getting the name Leslie or Printice, or both." Roberta laughed suddenly. It caught her and the doctor off-guard. Thankfully, none of her drink was spilled. "What's the joke?"

"Oh, nothing," she responded. "It must be this assignment I am working on. You see, I am a journalist by profession, and these days, I have been working on a story about abortion when it was legal. I was just thinking, so much of my sister's pregnancy, her child being conceived in rape, the life-threatening deformity, it being a girl . . . each of these things, by themselves, would have been enough to justify an abortion back then."

"Oh, I see," said the doctor without tensing up or worrying that someone around them might hear their conversation. "I take it you were thinking about a doctor's perspective."

"It can be off the record," she said, lightheartedly.

"Well," he began, the two slowly walking down the hall, "when I first started out here, I knew a few older nurses and surgeons who remembered those days. They were very apologetic about it, very much regretted that it used to happen, adamant about how awful abortion is, etcetera. A part of me always questioned their sincerity. Did they really hate abortion that much, or were they just saying that to avoid harassment?"

"I see," said Roberta, finishing off her cup of coffee as they paced to and from, the doctor not being needed at that point in his shift.

"I mean, I try to be fair," he continued. "I remind myself that medical technology wasn't as advanced back then; they didn't know as much about the unborn baby as we do now; and they didn't have as many resources. And yet, I also know that they still had plenty of information on in-utero development; they knew it was human; they still had exceptional medical technology back then and plenty of resources. People knew it was wrong. So, in my opinion, they have no excuse. They are all guilty."

"A collective punishment?"

"Well, I do not know," admitted the doctor. "I just know that in the hundreds of times that I have delivered babies—looking at that new, beautiful child—it never once occurred to me to kill it." As soon as he finished his declaration, the doctor received an alert about a patient. He looked down at the message on his digital pager, confirmed receipt of the message, and then looked up at Roberta. "Duty calls, as they used to say."

"Take care," she said, as he nodded and rushed off, leaving the journalist to ponder how to approach a beloved public figure who may have committed unthinkable acts.

. . . . . .

"Who's next?" asked Senator Benjamin Pettus, sitting on a black stool in a studio. He was wearing the usual three-piece suit with tie. Three automatic cameras were filming him from different angles. A black background was chosen for each of the recordings because the campaigns wanted the attention to stay on Senator Pettus. A director in casual fashion sat behind the lens, with a few staffers standing on either side.

"Senator Collins," responded Benjamin' executive assistant.

"Senator Collins," he affirmed.

"Ready, Senator Pettus?" asked the director.

He took a breath and gave a thumbs up.

"Okay then, same script as before," noted the director. "In three, two, one . . ." Lights on the cameras all turned from red to green as he briefly pointed at Benjamin. The elder statesman was a professional and immediately went into his comments.

"Hello, I am Senator Benjamin Pettus and I would like to offer my endorsement of Senator Genevieve Collins," began Benjamin, rarely blinking as he faced the center camera. "I have worked with Mrs. Collins for years on Capitol Hill. I know her to be an excellent representative for the great people of Kansas and for the nation at large. She has been a strong proponent of helping the less-fortunate and has consistently voted in favor of the healthcare law. So, I am calling upon all Kansan voters—liberal and conservative, man and woman—to come together and support my good friend Genevieve this November."

"All right. And scene!" shouted the director, the camera lights turning from green to red. "That was pretty good. But I would like you to do it two more times, just in case."

"Sure," said Benjamin.

"And make sure he says it while doing a handstand," shouted a familiar voice off camera. Benjamin smiled when he discovered the man behind the voice.

"Anwar!" he said thrillingly, getting up from the stool as the senator from New Jersey approached from the shadows.

"Okay, take five," stoically stated the director, getting up from his chair to go to the break room.

"How are you doing, Benjamin?"

"Pretty good," he said as the two stood between two of the cameras. Their lights were automatically shut down when the break was called.

"Filming more endorsements?"

"What can I tell you? My name isn't poison just yet," Benjamin said in a pleasant mood.

"Just don't accidentally endorse my opponent, okay?"

"Of course not," he said and laughed. "What brings you here?"

"Just wanted to give you the good news personally."

"What good news?"

"I'm ahead in the polls," said Anwar.

"Really?"

"The latest came out this morning," began the younger senator. "I now hold a comfortable lead over Nagar." Anwar took out his smart-phone and showed his friend the data.

"Well, beyond the margin of error, not bad."

"Thanks," he said as he put away his phone. "I also saw that you are doing well in the polls."

"I was always doing well in the polls."

"Yeah, but even better than earlier—you know, when that whole crazy conspiracy stuff was going around the blogosphere."

"Oh, yes, I remember," said Benjamin, adjusting his tie a little. "It astounds me just how kooky the internet can be."

"Definitely," nodded Anwar. "My grandfather used to tell me all sorts of stories about how when he was young, all sorts of hateful dangerous garbage used to fill up all the websites. Comment sections were especially bad, like a tornado, you know?"

"Yeah, I vaguely remember when it was still that way. That must make me . . . "

"Older than dirt?"

"Quiet you," lightly responded Benjamin, whose mood remained positive throughout the day and the remainder of the filming of his endorsement messages.

. . . . . .

Michael Chan was pacing around a walkway narrowed by cubicle walls. He was about twenty feet from an office door that was ajar. It was a place of fear. His stomach was troubled. Under his arm was a thin laptop with the information he hoped to convey. He wore his best wrinkled, collared shirt and properly trimmed his neck beard. An unwelcomed rival appeared from out of one of the open spaces.

"Well, I see a citizen journalist is in our midst," said Andrew McClellan, mockingly emphasizing the phrase "citizen journalist" in his sentence. "I am surprised trumpets did not announce your coming."

"I really am not in the mood, McClellan," said the visitor, getting some sincere hesitation on the part of the trolling reporter.

"Oh, I see; you have a meeting with Jocelyn. Job interview?"

"You wish. It's about a story."

"Is that the one Roberta has been working on all this time?"

"Yes," said the nervous Chan. "We both worked on it."

"Uh-huh," noted McClellan. "Well, I got to get back to work. You take care of yourself and go forth in your citizen journaling." With a mock salute, McClellan turned around and returned to his desk.

Chan was waiting for Roberta Sheridan to arrive. It felt like she was taking longer than expected. Maybe it was all sensation and not an actual indicator of the objective passage of time. Chan looked at his smartphone and confirmed that time was not moving as quickly as he hoped. Sheridan had mentioned working on another assignment that morning. Perchance, it was taking longer than previously assumed. He knew she was there, as they had briefly said hello several minutes earlier. A faint wave, a blinking acknowledgement. Then back to the assignment. She was a professional. He admired her for that sentiment. His nerves gave some ease when Sheridan finally reappeared.

"Ready, Berta?"

"Yeah." She nodded after a breath. As they entered Jocelyn Lopez's office, Chan could almost hear, "Trust in the Lord; He will deliver you. Have faith in the Lord, and He will see you through" rapidly spoken under her breath.

Lopez was as she often was, quietly overseeing various projects on two screens. For a split second, she saw the two people enter her office, giving a quick nod that implied both a greeting and an offer to take a seat. Chan followed the actions of his friend, sitting down on the other side of the desk as the Politics Department editor shut down both of the screens, the projections disappearing. Her uncorrupted attention came to the duo. Chan's nerves subsided as the action commenced, the battle of words beginning.

"Okay, Roberta, Chan," she said. "I wanted to meet with both of you because I am concerned that this story is taking too much time away from more important pieces, and honestly, I think it lacks enough evidence to be published. Simply put, prove me wrong."

Chan took the initiative. "Well, first of all, we have an eyewitness. Etna Lee worked along with Dr. Hood, and she was the one who reached out to me confirming that Senator Pettus is, in fact, Dr. Hood. Berta—that is, Sheridan here—she talked with Lee and found her credible."

"That's right," interjected Sheridan. "She was very sincere."

"Sincere doesn't equal right," rebutted Lopez. "It is her word against an established, widely respected politician. Did she have any factual evidence backing up her claims?"

"Um, no, not technically."

"Any other witnesses?"

"Not to my knowledge," conceded Sheridan.

"Mrs. Grant," declared Chan, prompting both Sheridan and Lopez to look at him. "Mrs. Grant backs up Lee. Says she's a credible witness."

"But Grant herself was not there and did not make the connection between Hood and Pettus, even though she has seen and met Pettus on multiple occasions."

"True, but she gives credence to Lee's claims."

"Not good enough."

"We also have letters," stressed Chan, who pushed a button on his laptop that created a screen and, with a few strokes, brought up multiple documents that were scanned into his machine a few days ago. He handed the small laptop to the editor. "These were fan letters sent to Linda Harrison, the hacker behind the Ultralord Virus. Sheridan and I think at least one of them was written by Pettus—that is, Dr. Hood—years back."

"None of them are signed," stated Lopez. "How do you know they were written by Pettus?"

"Well, obviously, some forensic science might be of help."

"This is not a crime lab," rebutted Lopez, pushing the button that dematerialized the screen and handing the device back to Chan. "And this is not enough."

"Mrs. Lopez—"

"Mr. Chan," stated the editor. "This is not enough to prove that Pettus and Hood are the same person. Do you have anything else? What about the plastic surgeons?"

"Nothing definitive," admitted Sheridan. "However, I am still waiting for some responses. If I keep up with them, I may be able to—"

"No."

"No?" asked a disappointed Chan. "You're saying no? As in, no more work?"

"I gave Sheridan and you plenty of time, several months in fact, to explore this potential lede. You have found some interesting evidence, but none of it proves that these two people are the same person. *The Kensington Post* is a widely respected news publication. We are not about to publish a conspiracy theory. This is not some stupid, extremist, rightwing blog."

That last comment infuriated Chan. He stood with an angered look and, rather than give more argument, exited the office with a suppressed rage. Sheridan looked at her editor with disappointment, turned to see her friend leaving in disgust, and went after him. McClellan saw the rival leave with head down and temper fuming, amused by the expression yet maintaining silence out of faint empathy. Roberta caught up with Michael after he pushed past the glass doors of that level's offices and cubicles.

"Mike, Mike," she said to grab his attention, prompting him to stop and face her.

"A stupid, extremist blog—that's my life's work she's talking about."

"She was just trying to protect our publication from scandal. She's critical like that; she has to be. Don't blame her, Mike. She has to answer to people, too."

"I'll show her. I'll show all your elitist friends. McClellan, Lopez, all of them," he said, pacing in his ire. "I'll publish what we have on Chan Worldwide News. It will be my publication's big break. And she'll be sorry."

"Mike, listen," began Roberta, slowing his pace. "Lopez has a point. It's not definite. We need more. And you need *The Post's* platform if you really want the world to see what you helped accomplish."

Michael shook his head. "Your editor said no. And the election is a month away. Someone has to expose Pettus for what he really is. I can do that."

"How? I have most of the interview content."

"Give it to me, and I'll write it up." Trying to lighten the mood, he added, "I'll even name you as a coauthor, if you like."

"Mike," she began, taking a breath before laying down the news. "I am not going to give you my interviews for your post."

"Are you kidding me, Berta? This is . . . this is unbelievable! This is pathetic!"

"It's journalism," she declared. "I agree with Lopez's criticism. And I am drawing the line here. I cannot let you do this."

"So, that's it?" he stated in anger. "That is eight months of work all gone?"

"No, it's not," insisted Roberta, stopping the slowed pacing of her friend by having a hand touch each shoulder. She looked him in his eyes. "Just give me some more time. I will think of something."

"What? What will you do?"

"I don't know yet."

"This is ridiculous . . ."

"Mike, Mike," she insisted. "Please. Please give me time. I will think of something. Somehow, some way, I will find an answer."

"How? How can you?"

"Pray for me."

Michael slowly nodded. "I'll be praying, all right. For you, for this story, for it all."

"Thank you," she said with renewed patience. The two embraced, and then Michael left, leaving Roberta feeling like she had taken a few punches to the head.

. . . . . .

Roberta Sheridan was having a miserable day. It was not because of an argument with a co-worker, nor was it over a correction that had to be issued or finding some criticism of her work on another website. Outside pressures were fairly light that day, no worse than an average shift. Rather, the suffering came from within. Congested nostrils, a scratchy throat, and a gnawing headache plagued the reporter. She struggled to labor on her stories, her eyes sensitive to the projected screen, even when set on a calmer image coloration. She frequently had to look away, pushing her fingers to her temples and forehead. She felt the strong pulsing of her blood when her digits touched the sides of her face.

Fortunately, her workload was not especially heavy, and her appetite was still present, with lunch being eaten without trouble. Still, even her ergonomic office chair was not sufficiently comforting to ease her ill feelings. During some downtime between stories, Andrew McClellan showed up, walking from his nearby cubicle to hers. He was in a good mood, which somehow made her feel worse. Then again, it was not as aggravating as the stare-down with the computer screen, so she accepted it.

"I know you told me you weren't a big fan of Charolash, but I thought you would be interested in joining us," insisted McClellan. "There are going to be a couple of local bands that might interest you."

"I like to buy local foods, not listen to local bands."

"Maybe you will like the local bands. They are more traditional rock, after all."

"Is one of them the praise band from my church?"

"Not to my knowledge."

"Then no, thank you," replied Roberta. "Besides, the way I feel right now, the last thing I want to do is go out tonight."

"I was about to say, what's the matter, and is it contagious?" asked her co-worker, feigning fear of infection.

"Obviously, it is not contagious," she said with an amused roll of her eyes. "It is just something seasonal. But it is still getting on my nerves."

"I'm surprised you didn't bring any uberpirin with you?"

"I forgot it on the way out the door. Do you have any?"

"Not here," said McClellan. "After all, I'm not sick."

"Yeah, not sick. I'd like that."

"Well, I'll ask around."

"Thanks," said Roberta as her co-worker turned away and started to inquire of the matter with their mutual acquaintances at *The Kensington Post.* She swung around in her chair to face the dreaded screen. There was still one more news article to write up that day before her assignments were completed. Just a mere five hundred to six hundred words separated her from the end of her burdens for that day. From there, perchance she would be able to get off early, make the public transportation journey back to her apartment, and from there get relief through a mixture of uberpirin, rest, and ample fluids.

"Hey," stated a feminine voice, prompting Roberta to turn around and behold a respectful and reserved Jocelyn Lopez. The editor gave the reporter a faint smile and a fainter nod.

"Hey," said the reporter to the editor, this being their first in-person conversation since the meeting with Michael Chan.

"Andrew said you were feeling sick."

"Yeah. Something seasonal."

"Here," Lopez directed, handing Sheridan a small, white bottle. "Take a couple of uberpirin."

"I didn't know you had any."

"I am an editor," stated Lopez with a light matter of fact tone. "I always keep at least one bottle at the office."

"Makes sense," conceded Roberta as she twisted off the cap and gently shook out two pills. "Thank you."

"No problem," said Lopez. She looked down briefly in silence before continuing. "You know, I feel I owe you an apology for yesterday. I probably should not have been so firm with Chan and you."

"Oh, that's okay," assured Roberta as she handed the closed bottle back to her editor. "We had it coming."

"Still, I want you to know that I was far angrier with Chan than with you. I know you know better, and I know you understood where I was coming from before things got heated. I just felt that he needed that firm rejection more than you."

"Probably," stated Roberta, who then placed one of the pills in her mouth and swallowed. She was always good at that, never needing a liquid to get it down.

"If you need to leave early, I can see to getting Suarez to do your last piece."

"No, no," assured Roberta as she put the second pill by her keyboard. "With the uberpirin and five or ten minutes of rest, I'll be back to normal."

"Okay," nodded Lopez. "Keep up the good work." With that last positive comment, the editor exited the cubicle and returned to her busy office.

Roberta was able to feel the pill taking effect, with the pressure on her brain beginning to ebb. She leaned back into her office chair, the furniture conforming to her demands and staying in the arched back status. Slowly, she closed her eyes and felt a growing sense of relief. She was feeling better about her relationship with her boss as well, for the two had failed to talk to one another the day before following the meeting. Just a brief goodbye as the shift ended. Sheridan had had issues with her editor before. Like any long-term friendship, there were times of awkwardness and argumentation. Mending always followed, even when it was not taken as assumed by the ailing journalist.

Buzzing noises disrupted her ease, making her ache that much more. In grimaced annoyance, she checked her computer screen to behold an announcement that she was being called. Recovering from the shock, she decided to answer the call rather than ignore it. However, given her mood, she chose the audio-only option for the communication, tapping the enter button on her keyboard twice once the mouse icon was on that box. She kept to her eased posture, the chair still largely horizontal. She closed her eyes once more, thinking that the communication was not going to be long or substantive.

"Roberta Sheridan, *Kensington Post*," she stated, formally.

"Oh, hello, Ms. Sheridan," said a cheerful woman on the other end. "This is Kelsey with Premium Cosmetic Surgeons of Baltimore, Maryland. Remember me?"

"Yes, actually, I do," she said, opening her eyes and looking at the screen on instinct, even though it was still audio-only. "How are you?"

"Fine, fine," she said. "I remember you contacted me awhile back about some story you were working on about Dr. Hood. I told you we were still organizing our files from that time period. Anyway, we're a long way from finishing up everything, but the other day we stumbled on some files that had the name Hood on them. I am emailing you a copy of them now." Roberta readjusted her chair and got to a more professional posture. With curious eyes, she checked her work email and saw that a new message had come into her inbox. The email had an attachment. "Did you get the email?"

"Yes," she answered. "I am looking at it now."

"Okay, I just wanted to see if this is what you were looking for." Roberta's eyes widened with shock and success. She kept looking at it, skimming each important point rapidly and repeatedly. A great, big smile spread across her face. Maybe it was the advanced modern aspirin taking full effect, but she realized it was much more than that. She nearly forgot to respond. A patient voice interrupted her euphoria. "Does it help your article?"

"Oh, yes. Very."

"That's great," Kelsey said. "Is there anything else I can do for you?"

"Oh, no, this is plenty. Thank you so much. Thank you so very much."

"No problem. Well, if you need anything else, feel free to give us a call."

"All right, I will. Have a good day and thank you again."

"Yes, bye."

CHAPTER 9

ROBERTA SHERIDAN STUDIED HER EDITOR while she waited for any response of any kind. Roberta was seated crossed-legged with hands over her lap as she remained silent in patience. Her positioning was on the other side of the desk from Jocelyn Lopez, who had not looked at the reporter for the past three minutes. Roberta did not want to interrupt, she did not dare to make any added comments, lest it sway the mood away from her goals. So she sat there, in the most cautious of optimisms.

Lopez continued to stoically review the printed materials before her. There were five pages altogether. They included doctor's notes on how the procedure was going to be performed, a memorandum on specific facial adjustments. There were illustrations, showing the before and the after according to the plans. Photos were lacking, but fingerprints and an infamous signature were present. A date was also listed, one from decades previous. The papers were authentic, and their source was valid.

Roberta kept looking, her anxiety neither growing nor shrinking. Her examination of her editor noted all the finer points. When Lopez was tacitly studying something, her lips faintly parted, then slowly increased the gap to show teeth before they closed. She always licked her thumb in a quick motion before moving a printed page to the back of the line. Then she stacked the pages a few times on the desktop to keep them in relative order. Then more silence in her reviewing of the text.

"It's the perfect trap," suddenly declared Lopez, causing Roberta to shift in her chair. The editor looked up at the reporter, still holding up the pages. "It's the perfect trap."

Roberta had no idea what this twice-uttered statement entailed. Both times, Lopez declared it with firm confidence. Both times, Roberta was unsure as to what was meant. In the moments of silence that followed the repeat of the sentence, a flurry of thoughts and possibilities entered Roberta's mind. A trap for whom? How was it perfect? There was no spoiling of the argument, no tell in the glance of the superior. Just no blinking, no flinching, no hesitation. A surety followed the next several sentences.

"We contact Senator Benjamin Pettus about what we have found. We inform him that we are going to publish this document, along with the other information you have gathered over the past nine months. If he does not want us to publish it, the only way he can legally stop us would be to acknowledge that these are his medical records. If he says nothing or allows us to publish this document, then the general public will see that right before Pettus became a known figure, the American Mengele underwent surgery that, according to these records, made him look exactly like Pettus, right down to his fingertips. No matter what, Pettus will admit that he is none other than Dr. Edgar Hood," explained Lopez, pausing for a moment before making a familiar declaration. "It is the perfect trap."

Roberta was welling up with a new happiness, fueling the joy she felt earlier that day when she received the proof her investigative piece needed. The decision was becoming more evident, and yet Lopez spelled it out nonetheless, adding further information to confirm the victory: "That is why we are going to run your story when it is finished and give it big attention. It will be prominent on the main page and at the top of the emailed newsletter. We will make sure the whole country knows about this before the midterms."

"And Michael Chan will be given credit for his contributions?" she said, her joyousness arousing a new audacity.

"Yes, sure. I guess we owe him, after all," conceded the editor.

"Thank you, I will let him know."

"Before anything else happens, though," cautioned Lopez with a raised hand, "you need to reach out to Pettus. Call his office, call his campaign, call any other number and message any email address you have. Make an extra effort to get his response."

"Yes, ma'am."

"We are the ones who have time on our side for a change. He will know that. So do what you can to get his perspective."

"Yes."

. . . . . .

"I'm so glad I listened to you," said Michael, his face projected on the digital screen.

"You should do so more often," Roberta responded with a grin.

"I might," he conceded. "So, what is the next step?"

"Contacting Pettus. See what he has to say."

"I doubt he has a good answer," said Michael, who added, "not as good as the answer Helen gave when I popped the question."

"Must you remind me," Roberta joked. "You're making me feel old."

"Not intended," he said with palms raised. "Anyway, keep up the good work. I guess my prayers were answered. Bye!"

"Bye," she said, ending their face-to-face tele-correspondence.

Roberta directed her phone application to search for contact information on Senator Benjamin Pettus. A search of her records did not locate the proper contact information for the senator's office or his campaign. She minimized the application and opened a web page. After checking her work email, she opened a new tab to search for the necessary number. Sure enough, Pettus' official page included a press contact. The reporter copied and pasted the number into the phone application and clicked enter.

"Hello?" asked a woman on the other end of the audio-only communication.

"Hello, is this Alicia Tamer?"

"This is she. How can I help you?"

"My name is Roberta Sheridan, and I am a reporter with *The Kensington Post*. I am working on a story about Senator Benjamin Pettus and wanted to touch base."

"Okay," responded Tamer. "What's your story about?"

"Well," began Roberta, seeking to be civil in her discourse. "I am researching Pettus' background for a news story. I wanted the senator to review some of the things I found and provide some clarifications."

"Okay. What did you find?" asked the curious spokesperson.

"Let me email it all to you. It would be better if you read it."

"Okay, sure."

"I can send the email through this number, correct?"

"Of course."

"Okay then," replied Roberta. "I will send you something in a few minutes."

"All right. I will see to getting it to Senator Pettus as soon as possible. Do you have a deadline?"

"Preferably by tomorrow morning."

"Okay," said Tamer in an upbeat mood. "I will send your stuff along to Senator Pettus, and he should have a response for you by the end of the day."

"That's good to hear. Thank you."

"Anything else?"

"No, that will do it. I will send it to you immediately."

"Okay, thank you."

"Bye!"

"Goodbye."

Roberta tapped the end button, and the phone conversation was concluded. She returned to her work email, deleted several list serv messages that were not newsworthy or germane to her assignments, and then opened a new email for sending to Tamer. The number was pasted into the recipient bar, a title for the message was written in all-caps for that respective bar, and then the body of the email featured a short comment about the attached contents. From there, Roberta attached the body of her evidence: the interview with Etna Lee, the interview with Clara Grant, the letters to the hacker that seemed to have been authored by the senator, and, most notably, the plastic surgery paperwork.

The next day, Roberta had received no response from Pettus or his spokesperson by the time her shift ended. It was midmorning, and nothing had been sent via email or phone call. Having finished submitting a different article, Roberta clicked on the phone application and called up the press contact. It rang three times before a voice answered: "Hello?"

"Good morning, this is Alicia Tamer, right?"

"Right," she cautiously responded.

"This is Roberta Sheridan with *The Kensington Post*. I talked with you yesterday about an article I was working on about Senator Pettus and his background."

"Oh, right. Yes, I remember."

"You told me that you were going to have a response for me by the end of the day. I just wanted to make sure that your message wasn't lost in my junk file or something."

"Oh, no, it wasn't," assured Tamer. "Pettus has been very busy with a debate on the federal budget, and so I didn't get a chance to show him what you sent me."

"Okay," replied Roberta, opting to give some benefit of a doubt to the spokeswoman. "Understood. Do you know when he will have a chance to respond?"

"I know he will for sure look at it today. If I have to, I'll print it all out and shove it in his face," she said, following it with laughter. "But he will see it today. However, I do not believe he will have time to respond by the end of the day."

"Okay," the journalist replied. "Do you know when he will be able to respond?"

"Probably by the end of the week," answered Tamer, who quickly followed up with, "does that work for your deadline?"

"It should, yes," bluffed Roberta, who knew she did not have an official deadline. "I look forward to hearing back from the senator soon."

"I will see what I can do."

"Thank you."

"Anything else you need? The senator recently took some official photos, so if your news publication needs new images of him, we can give them today."

"No, that's okay. We have plenty of recent ones in our system."

"Okay, then. Have a good day!"

"You, too. Bye."

It was the following Monday, with the outside already getting dark. This was due to the decreasing hours of sunlight and an approaching thunderstorm, whose clouds dominated the heavens. The blast of lightning and heavy rains was set to counter the day-long heat and humidity that early autumn in the metropolitan area was known to express. The other assignments were completed. One of them, to Roberta's amusement, was a quick update on the polling data for the senatorial race in Virginia. Pettus was still well ahead of Gutierrez, with every expert predicting a swift re-election. If only they knew what was going to hit the presses once her article was completed.

"Hello?"

"Hi, Alicia, this is Sheridan with *The Kensington Post.*"

"Oh, hi," said the cautious voice.

"Just wanted to check on things."

"Yes, that," began Tamer. "Senator Pettus has read what you sent, but he cannot respond today. More budget debates and some campaign stops are in the way."

"Understood," said the reporter, who doubted the response. "Would it be possible for him to respond by the end of this week?"

"Honestly, this whole month is pretty bad for him. What with the campaign and Capitol Hill stuff, he does not have a lot of free time. He might be able to respond next month. I can check his availability if you like."

"That would be appreciated, sure," kindly responded an impatient Roberta.

"Anything else I can help you with?"

"Actually, one more thing," stated Roberta, committed to her job. "Can you please let Senator Pettus know that my article is going to run soon, regardless of whether or not he responds?"

"Sure, I can tell him that."

"Good, thank you."

"Bye!" said Tamer, hanging up before Roberta could say the same.

The following morning was cooler. Aside from last night's thunderstorm, scattered showers hit Maryland and the District of Columbia in the early morning. Vegetation glistened, sidewalks were darkened, and the air was a tad cold. Roberta was about to enter the building. She had talked with Michael Chan yesterday about the article. He was adamant about the need to get it published before it was too late; Roberta assured him that they still had more than a month before election day. She said her usual greetings to the folks on the first floor, getting to an open elevator. The lift was all hers, the lone passenger whose silent journey upward was interrupted by a ringing phone. Taking it from her purse, the screen had an orange tint, indicating that it was work-related.

"Hello?" asked Roberta, the number being unsaved.

"Pettus will speak with you in person this coming Friday at ten in the morning," stated Tamer as though giving an order. "You will meet him at his home in Alexandria, Virginia. I will email you the address."

. . . . . .

Roberta Sheridan decided to take the bus that morning. Pettus' home was very close to a bus stop, on a route that began at the Pentagon. The forty-foot long bus she took was completely automated. The routes were in the system, with the doors opening once the vehicle halted at the stop. A pull of the cord above informed the computer of the need for a rider to get off of the vehicle. Passengers paid at a machine located right at the door, using a fare card, debit or credit card, or cash. All who entered had their photo taken, and the stop they get off at recorded, allowing for authorities to track down those who tried to duck paying the fare. Sometimes, a human being rode along for maintenance or security reasons.

The bus did not have many occupants. It was after the morning rush, and they were going the opposite direction of most D.C. area workers. Sheridan had that point made at the Pentagon bus area, when she saw about thirty people disembark from the bus she would use to get to suburban Alexandria. Only twice was the bus halted to have commuters disembark. Amid the large family houses and towering spreading trees, Sheridan got closer and closer to her destination. She quickly observed from her mobile phone screen that she was set to get to the house of the interviewee sooner than scheduled. It was a minor concern. The brevity of the situation served that purpose.

As the automated vehicle went down Cameron Mills, nearing on one side an old church building, Sheridan kept wondering why she felt those pits of dread in her midsection. She knew she was right. She knew he was who she and Michael Chan had long expected him to be. Her editor—the critical, objective Jocelyn Lopez—agreed as well. She was puzzled by the innate fretting. Maybe she feared retribution. He was powerful, after all. An online lynch mob, a physical lynch mob, legions of misguided blind partisans who would never believe anything if their political deities told them not to.

Sheridan thought more about the impact, the unintended consequences, and the uncertainty of what she was entering. That had to be it, the source of the worry. She was fairly sure that an interview was what she was traveling toward. However, maybe it was something else. Maybe a meeting with his lawyers, an in-person threat of physical harm. The panic scenarios were getting absurd, and objectively speaking, she knew them to be just that. Yet there was always the pondering idea. After all, what she had was destined to cause great political upheaval and likely shift the direction of the country. It was such that she nearly forgot to pull the cord for her stop, successfully doing a mere two blocks from the destination.

The machine got the message and properly slowed to a stop with exact precision. The front portion kneeled, and the doors opened, a speaker confirming the name of the stop. Sheridan smiled and nodded at the human employee, who sat just behind the hardware of the digital mind guiding the bus. The reporter walked down the three steps, the bottom one lowered so the vehicle touched the sidewalk. Two seconds after she was clear of the steps, the doors behind her shut, and the automated bus pulled away from the stop and eventually sped off, keeping to a proper schedule with little variance.

Sheridan looked around the locale. It was peaceful; no one seemed to be around. No surprise, given that it was during the work day. To her right was a four-way intersection, each side getting a stop sign, with a blinking red light suspended above the middle square. Behind her and before her were small homes with fences. To her left was an elementary school with a vegetable garden based in front of one of the classroom wings. Otherwise, it had a large, cleanly cut green lawn split by a broad sidewalk that led to the main entrance. Another thinner sidewalk came in from the parking lot to the right of the school building, eventually connecting to the aforementioned broad sidewalk.

No cars coming from either side, Sheridan walked across the street without going to the proper pedestrian walkway outlined about twenty feet to her right. Once on the other side, she turned right, and then upon getting to the intersection, turned left to get onto Virginia Avenue. A block later, she came across another inter-section with four stop signs but no flashing red lights. She took out her phone from her purse to verify the address, with the phone GPS showing with moving arrow where she had to go next. A left onto Taylor Avenue, the destination being to her right. The school park-ing lot was in front of her as she turned.

"Trust in the Lord; He will deliver you," she said to herself, a vol-ume above whisper as no one was around. "Have faith in the Lord; He will see you through."

The house was new, though it was based off of an earlier structure. It was the only home among the collection at the dead-end street that had a fence, and one made of well-cut wood. As she went by the other homes, she noticed that two of them had small, cubic-shaped automated mowers cutting their lawns. Most models could be programmed by the owner to trim the grass at certain times of the week and year. Recent ones were even coming out that could be automatically triggered to do the chore five minutes after the owner left for work. The technology was normative enough that forcing minors to mow the lawn was deemed a form of child abuse in some localities in the United States, plus a few European countries.

Security was stationed at the gate of the fence. As Roberta neared it, the two personnel standing there beckoned her to stop within a few feet of the fence. A third man was standing behind the two personnel. He was at the entrance to the house, under an awning supported by two decorative beams. One of the two folks at the gate spoke up: "Name and ID, please."

"I am Roberta Sheridan, reporter with *The Kensington Post*," she said as she untucked her lanyard from her light jacket and held it up. "I have an interview with Senator Pettus scheduled for 10:00 a.m. I admit, I am a little early."

"I see," said one of the two security personnel. "I am going to confirm this. Wait here." He turned away and talked quietly into a small device based in his sleeve. Meanwhile, the other security personnel took out a tennis ball-sized instrument and used it to scan Sheridan for any possible weapons. He moved it a few inches up and down in the air to help get a full analysis. He nodded without speaking as he put away the device. The other man returned to the gate shortly after. "Okay, Ms. Sheridan, you are free to enter."

"Thank you," she said meekly, as one of the two opened the gate for her to enter the front yard. As Sheridan walked closer to the front door, she saw the third security figure step out of the protection of the awning and go to the side. Before her, the main door pulled open, with only the screen door separating outside from in.

Senator Benjamin Pettus was exuding a friendly demeanor as he showed up from behind the opened door. The elder statesman had pearly white teeth, kind eyes, and a proper suit with a dark blue tie. As Sheridan neared the awning, he opened the screen door, its glass and brown metal frame pushing forward. The reporter gently caught the edge of the door with her left hand and held it open for herself as he talked. "Good morning, Ms. Sheridan! Welcome to my home. Did your trip from D.C. go well?"

"It was faster than usual."

He laughed as she entered the hallway of the home. "Well, that's what happens when you go one way while everyone else goes the other." He laughed again. She could tell there was some nerves in him, too. That realization calmed any apprehension. Just before veering left into the living room, he stopped. "You interviewed me once before, right?"

"Yes, I did," answered Sheridan. "Back in January. On Capitol Hill."

"Oh, that's right; I remember now," he said. "First session of the year." He laughed again. "It seems like it was a long time ago."

"Very long," she agreed, prompting a little more laughter from the elected official. As they got into the living room, Roberta viewed the life around her. An artificial fireplace on the opposite end. Photos of him, his wife, his children, and their children sat on two mantles and above the fireplace. Comfy chairs were situated at certain points, and two black bookshelves stood at opposite corners, filled with various hardback and paperback books. Green carpeting showed some wear from personal history, but new wallpaper decorated on all sides. A large window was positioned to her left, with curtains closed but that offered a view of the school, the lot, the security, and the neighbors. Roberta was in a personal setting. It was the environment she expected for such a conversation as the one she sought to have, on the record, for the very public news piece.

"Would you like something to drink? Coffee? Orange juice?"

"I am all right, thank you."

"Have a seat," offered Pettus. Roberta took one that was adjacent to a three-foot tall mantel piece. It would be ideal to place her recorder. He sat in the chair on the other side of the mantel, his veneer of welcoming slowly entering into unwanted business. "Now, then, um, to your story," he said with ominousness. "Just so you know, I read the information that you sent my press person, and I would like to respond."

"All right," said Roberta, who took out her digital recorder from her purse and placed it on the mantel. She was about the push the record button with her index finger when the senator spoke up.

"Before we go on the record, however, I wanted to 'introduce' you to a few people," he began, with Roberta agreeing to not push the button. Pettus had his own small device, square-shaped, which he put on the other end of the mantel top. He pressed a couple of buttons, and a holographic video image of an African-American woman appeared, her projected body being about fifteen inches tall.

"This is Damaica. She was a single mother who worked two jobs to provide for her three kids. Neither job provided healthcare benefits. Damaica's daughter Sheila became gravely ill and needed surgery. Sheila would have died, but thankfully, because of my healthcare law, Damaica was able to pay for the procedure. Sheila not only survived, but also grew up to become a successful business owner who gives back to the community."

Roberta folded her arms as he pushed a button that caused the projected woman to vanish. A couple of more hits on the device and the senator had another woman, a Caucasian this time, projected at about fifteen inches tall. "This is Haley. She was an army wife whose husband was killed in the war. Months after the funeral, she found out two disturbing things. The first was that with his passing, a loophole was triggered that ended her medical coverage. The second was that she had breast cancer, a potentially fatal illness back in those days. Fortunately, the federal healthcare law was able to lend a hand and give her the necessary coverage so that she could get the treatments she needed to beat cancer." A push of a button and Haley disappeared. He pushed a couple more things to bring up a third woman. She looked to be Latina, though it was not clearly evident. "This is Zoe—"

"I'm sorry, Senator Pettus," Roberta interjected. "I would like to know what this has to do with my story."

"Oh, of course, yes, of course," he began, turning off the projection and removing the device from the mantel, so that it could no longer interfere with the story. "The point I am trying to make is that a lot of people owe their lives to my work. To my healthcare law. I fight all day and all night to keep it on the books. My whole life, in fact, I have done everything I could to try and help people." He looked down. "Rightly or wrongly." Then he looked back toward the journalist, who perked up at the subliminal confession. "I have long wanted to help people who have been historically marginalized, oppressed, subjugated to second-class citizenry. I assume that a woman of color like yourself can appreciate that more than most." Roberta withheld judgment at the pandering. "As a doctor, I had to take an oath to do no harm." He briefly laughed. "I am unfamiliar with journalism school, but I am certain that professional journalists have a similar ethical obligation."

"True, there is a journalism standard for minimizing the harm to those we write about," acknowledged Roberta, getting a smile of relief from Pettus. "However, this protection from harm is meant more for private citizens than notable public figures, least of all one who has around-the-clock security. Furthermore, it is the obligation of a journalist to report the truth and to foster an informed populace." Each point was stressed, each sentence a blow to the comfort the senator was developing. "Now, Senator Pettus, I would like for you to go on the record and respond to what I have sent you." He looked down and nodded, leaning back into his chair as the reporter turned on the recording device. She directed her focus to him. "Now, Senator Benjamin Pettus, I would like to know in light of the evidence I sent you, are you, in fact, Dr. Edgar Hood, the infamous abortionist?"

"Yes," he said with surprisingly little hesitation. "Yes, I am he. I am now called Benjamin Odin Pettus . . . but I was born Edgar Billings Hood of Boulder, Colorado. I was educated in Colorado and Maryland as a medical professional before accepting a position in California at the West Coast Clinic for Women. I performed thousands of abortions while on staff, most when the . . . when the baby was able to survive outside the womb. I eventually took control of the facility when I bought it from Dr. Hampton Lee, father of the nurse Etna Lee. When *Roe v. Wade* was overturned, I engaged in political activism in a failed attempt to keep abortion legal. When . . . when that did not work, I decided to disappear. I took out all my money from the bank, then purposely infected my records with the Ultralord Virus. Then I rebuilt my identity, taking various biographical information from people I knew growing up."

Roberta was witnessing the outflow of a confession. He said his comments with little blinking and with a weighed conscience. He spoke as a criminal finally caught by the police, as a man on the deathbed speaking of a long covered-up indiscretion. The patronizing was over; the authenticity was pouring forth. Her device recorded it all. Nevertheless, she took notes with a traditional pen and paper to highlight important parts. A strange habit to control her hands, for it seemed that all of what he said was important.

"Your research was very well done. I mean that. Etna told the truth about my background. Yes, I voted against that expanded language for the amnesty in the hopes of keeping her quiet. I assumed that was why she had not ratted me out when she first figured out who I was. And yes, I did ask Grant about plastic surgery clinics to help me change my appearance. I eventually settled on Premium Cosmetic Surgeons in Baltimore for my procedure. The papers you have were indeed signed by me and are about my surgery. I give you permission to release the documents for your story. I have only one correction—I never sent a letter to the Ultralord person. I was not that foolish."

"Then I will take note of that," she said.

"What else do you want to know?"

"Why politics?" Roberta asked. "Politics is a profession where a person is constantly scrutinized. If you wanted to disappear, you picked a strange occupation."

He gave a weak smile. "Well, I honestly did not believe anybody would find out my true identity. I underestimated the news industry, I guess," he said, with her nodding. "Really, it went back to my activism following the overturning of *Roe*. Some people talk about getting the 'acting bug.' Well, I got the activism bug. I wanted to do more in public policy, run for office. I had a master plan of sorts. I was going to . . . I was going to get elected to the U.S. Senate; and then, once in office, I was going to introduce a bill to legalize abortion. You know, do it the right way this time. Through the legislature, elected officials. That way, no sense of 'judicial tyranny' or broad, brutal fiat. I was even going to include some concessions, like a ban on late-term abortion, mandatory parental notification. Little things."

"Why didn't you?"

"Times had changed," he responded. "By the time I was elected, it was clear that society had moved on. Even Planned Parenthood was obeying the laws at that point. And with the amnesty, the widespread outrage over the practice, the general belief that it was 'settled law'— whatever that means—I never went through with my plan. However, I saw that there were other issues, other problems, things that I could help with. Having been a doctor for so many years, I knew about the problems with healthcare coverage, the many loopholes and flaws in the system. So I went about trying to fix that. I wanted that to be my ultimate, lasting legacy. I have always wanted to help people."

"Do you regret your previous life?" asked the journalist to the former abortionist.

"Every day," he stated. "A part of me always feared that this would happen. I dreaded the possibility, as I knew it was never fully impossible. But more than being caught, I regret the savagery, the sick things I used to do. It always troubled me, ripping apart a small human being. The blood, the flailing, the discarded limbs and organs. My mentors used to brush it off. They said I would get over it. One even went as far as to compare it to gallbladder surgery. Can you believe that? Gallbladder surgery? But no, I never got over it. There are still nightmares. My hands covered in blood, red fetuses surrounding me. The experimentation I used to do. I kept telling myself it was for the better. It was progress in action. Some progress. So, yes, Ms. Sheridan, I regret it all. I hope your readers understand that."

Roberta did not respond to the stated hope of her interviewee. She had more than enough to write the story. Everything necessary—the recorded audio and the already prepared transcription waiting to be downloaded to her computer. She pushed the button on the device, turning it off, and put it away. She stood up, her host remaining seated with his head down. "Thank you for taking the time to speak with me and for verifying my claims. I will be writing up the article this afternoon. I expect it will be published next Monday. It is against *Kensington Post* policy to send an interviewee an entire article in advance of its publication. However, I will email your press person, Tamer, a link to the story once it is released. If there are any errors, she can let me know, and I will forward her message to my editor."

He nodded weakly. Roberta was unsure what to say next. Normally, she would have a cordial goodbye with an interviewee. Yet, seldom was the subject of an interview like this one. Rarely did she ever leave an interview on such bad terms, even amid a recognized respect. She put her things in her purse and readied to leave. He was not looking, his gaze still downward. His expression solemn. His elbow rested on the mantel top, his hand supporting his forehead. In pity, she approached him.

"I know this was hard for you, and I am sorry," said the reporter, who began to leave the living room for the hallway.

"Miss Sheridan," he spoke up, prompting her to stop and turn to face him, still sitting by the mantel. "I hope you understand . . . when your article is published, you will be signing the death warrants of millions."

"No, Dr. Hood," Roberta stated firmly, suppressing much emotion. "You did that decades ago—when you first looked at a healthy baby in the womb . . . and decided that it should die."

Hood gave no further comment, nor any further protest. Roberta gave no further word and left the house without incident to do her job. Roberta did not look back; she could not bear doing so.

After the article was published, *Chan Worldwide News* garnered the largest monthly page views in its history, as well as a quintupling of its social media following. By the end of the year, Michael Chan was able to enter the Enemy of the People Club by himself.

Even with eventual publication and the strong electoral shift it created, Roberta always felt a pinch of guilt over what it cost a man whom she once respected. On that day, interview completed, she left him there, hunched over and in drear sentiment, trying harder and harder to figure out how, despite all of his best efforts, despite all the care and social conformity, he still ended up on "the wrong side of history."

THE END

a Spiral
INTO Marvelous
LIGHT

A NOVEL

Michael Gryboski

ALSO BY MICHAEL GRYBOSKI:
A SPIRAL INTO MARVELOUS LIGHT

For decades, the Reverend Sammy Milton was a force in American politics.

An outspoken leader of the Religious Right, Milton divided his time between evangelizing the lost and galvanizing conservative voters. His rhetoric was polarizing, his positions were divisive, and he garnered many enemies over the years. When news outlets carried word of his death, many openly expressed joy at his passing.

Scott Addison was a product of his time.

A liberal journalist working in the Nation's Capital, he cared little for religion one way or the other. He held, like so many of his peers, a thoroughly negative opinion of the infamous figure. On the day Milton died, Addison was assigned to write an in-depth story meant to bury the fundamentalist preacher in vitriol. He expected the piece to be an easy one.

However, as he talked with those who knew Milton, both friend and foe alike, Addison's image of the late preacher became more complicated.

Far from a simple assignment, the story would take him to places he never thought possible.

For more information about

Michael Gryboski
and
Memories of Lasting Shadows
please visit:

www.facebook.com/MichaelCGryboski
@MichaelGryboski
www.instagram.com/michaelgryboski
www.crossnation.tumblr.com

For more information about
AMBASSADOR INTERNATIONAL
please visit:

www.ambassador-international.com
@AmbassadorIntl
www.facebook.com/AmbassadorIntl

*If you enjoyed this book, please consider leaving us a review on
Amazon, Goodreads, or our website.*